Sisterhood

The Bonds of Sisterhood Book 2

William Dance

Sisterhood
Copyright © 2022 by William Dance

ISBN
978-1-959314-18-9 (Paperback)
978-1-959314-19-6 (eBook)

Sisterhood

Written by William Dance

TABLE OF CONTENTS

INTRODUCTION

When we last checked in on Cashmere, Tammy, Stephanie, and Char, they lived as best as possible. Some were living a glorious life; others were living life as they thought they should. So, Cashmere, Tammy, and Stephanie set sail on their trip as planned.

This is where we pick up from. First, take a gander at the pages of this book to see just how their trip turns out. Then, get ready to board these pages and see the adventure that these ladies will go on. Live their journey with them. Experience all that they will experience!

This vacation is everything that they had dreamed about for some time now. These ladies deserve to have the best time of their lives, and that's just what they intend to do.

There isn't a way to explain what these ladies will endure this time. Some will experience total happiness and accomplish their dreams. Yet, we will meet others with unfathomable loss and heartbreak.

What are you waiting for? Come on in and take a peek!

Chapter 1

The Diamond Line left the dock on day one, and the girls left the upper deck. They took a stroll around this vessel to check out all that was offered on this magnificent vessel. They walked until they saw an enormous pool. People are swimming and hanging out in it. There were lots of kids laughing and playing. Some people were hanging out, already having drinks and getting cozy.

The girls continued to walk around the boat. Then, finally, they ventured upstairs to find several restaurants, bars, a casino, and even two nightclubs. Cashmere looked at the others and said: "It's about to be on tonight in this piece!" Tammy looked at Cashmere, smiled, and said, "I know that's right, girl!" "I can't believe we are finally here. We've waited so long for this moment…" Stephanie said.

They walked by the ship's bridge and saw the Captain at the helm. He nodded at them, and they smiled back. Cashmere's phone notified her of a message. She checked her messages and saw something that made her curious. It was from Ingrid… "I don't mean to bother you, but call me when you get a chance." The first thing that came to Cashmere's mind was that something was wrong with her little sister. Cashmere wanted to text or call her but was too scared to do so. She feared the worst. She showed the phone to Stephanie… They both had concerned looks on their faces. Finally, Stephanie told Cashmere, "You need to contact her right now and see what is going on." "I know, but there is something eerie about her text. I am almost certain it is awful news." Cashmere said: "You will never know if you don't get in touch with her. If it is awful news, don't you think you should know sooner rather than later?" Chimed Stephanie. The bottom line was that Cashmere knew she needed to contact her. She was just worried about what Ingrid's response would be. Stephanie's face showed much frustration… "Call her now, Cashmere!"

Cashmere pulled up the text, read it once more, and pressed the phone button. The phone dialed, and Ingrid answered almost as instantly as the phone rang. "Cashmere…" Ingrid stated. "Cashmere…" she stated again. "Hey girl, how are you?" Cashmere said. "Well, to be honest, things could be better." "What do you mean, Ingrid? What's going on?" "Well, I am in the hospital." "Hospital… what's wrong, Ingrid." "I am in labor, and it doesn't look good." "Ingrid, what are you talking about?" "Cashmere, the baby is a breach, and it is premature. It's coming tonight, and the chances of survival are very slim." "Oh no, Ingrid. I am so sorry to hear that." Cashmere could hear the crack in Ingrid's voice. She knew she was about to cry. She knew she was about to lose it. All Cashmere could think was, I need to be there with my sister.

Cashmere ran back to the helm where she had last seen the Captain. When she got there, he was no longer in sight. She frantically knocked on the window. One of the crew members looked her way. She didn't hesitate to gesture for him to come to her. He walked over to the door, opened it, and said: "May I help you?" She answered before he could even get the last word out. "I need to get off of this ship. My sister is in labor, and things don't look well for the baby!" "Ma'am, we are out at sea. I am not sure what I can do for you." "Call your Captain; I don't have time to waste. I need to get to Virginia as soon as possible." "Ma'am… I will try to help you, but I'm not sure I can!" "Look… I will not repeat this! Call your damn Captain! Get him up here right now!" "What is going on here?" She turned around and saw the Captain standing right behind her. "Captain… I have a serious situation, and I desperately need your help." "Henderson… Captain Henderson at your service." Cashmere told the Captain of her sister's situation. He immediately commanded one of his crew members to contact the Coast Guard for a helicopter. "Ma'am, we normally don't do this thing, but my daughter just had a child, so I can understand what you are going through. We were on pins and needles ourselves." Cashmere looked out the window to see her girls outside. "Could you please let them in? They are with me." She said, "Well, we do not allow people in here unless they are part of the crew. Please tell me your name and stateroom. I will have one of my crew members come and get you a few minutes before the helicopter arrives." "My name is Cashmere, and I am in stateroom 323." "Okay, Ms. Cashmere, we will have someone contact you as soon as the helicopter is close. I ask that you remain in your stateroom until the helicopter arrives. That way, we are certain to get you off the ship ASAP!" "Captain Henderson, thank you so very much! I truly appreciate this." Cashmere turned and walked towards her girls. Captain Henderson admired her dedication to her sister. When Cashmere closed the helm door, her girls bombarded her with questions. They wanted to ensure she was okay and could go home. She quickly let them know that Captain Henderson was more than helpful and said he would send someone to get her when the helicopter was near. Then it dawned on all that Cashmere would not be experiencing the great vacation they had all planned. The important thing was making sure that Ingrid and the baby were okay. The girls walked towards the elevator; once they got there, Cashmere pushed the third floor button. Stephanie looked over at Cashmere and said, "Girl, everything will be okay. You will see once you get there." Her girls gave her a hug to show their support. "We got you!" Tammy said. "I know. I love you guys so much. This is my baby sister. If something happens to her baby, it will be rough on her!" "No, Cashmere, Ingrid is our baby sister too. If something happens to her, it will be rough on all of us!" stated Stephanie. Tears welled up in Cashmere's eyes. At this point, she remembered how close she and Stephanie were, despite all they had been through recently. Stephanie had always been a wonderful friend to her. That was probably what made her want to kiss her. If she would venture into a relationship with a woman, she knew Stephanie would be the one for her. When they exited the elevator, it was a short walk to her room. The girls came in; Tammy poured wine to ease their nerves. She knew Cashmere needed to relax and not think about Ingrid so much. She would have plenty of time to think about Ingrid and the baby when she arrived in Virginia. That would be the only thing she would have time to think about. No matter how many positive thoughts Stephanie tried to have, something told her there was more to this than what was being said. Maybe more than Cashmere knew about. Since she couldn't confirm that, all she could do was wait and pray for the best! The only thing any of them could do now was to leave it in GOD's hands.

Chapter 2

Unfortunately, the vacation they had been planning started with a twist. No one knew what was going on with Cashmere. She had left a few hours ago. Captain Henderson said he would let them know when the helicopter had arrived. They hadn't heard from him at all. They figured she hadn't landed yet. Tammy thought, at the least, she would have called them to let them know how things were going. She didn't want to worry Cashmere more, so she kept her thoughts to herself.

Finally, Tammy's phone chirped. She rushed to it to see Cashmere's text to her. When she saw the text, she smiled. It wasn't Cashmere; it was Rico texting to ensure she was okay. She couldn't hold her smile back. Her smile grew wider and wider. Stephanie noticed and said, "Girl, who is texting you? Never mind, it must be Rico!" "Yes, it is my baby. He texts to check on me. He says "hello to everyone." Tammy begins to text Rico about Cashmere and Ingrid. She tells him all about the baby.

"Babe, do you need me to do anything? Do you want me to go to the hospital and keep her company until Cashmere arrives?" Before answering, Tammy thought about what he had just asked. He knew Ingrid, but she didn't think he knew her well enough to make that offer. His offer seemed as if he knew her more than she thought he knew her. As if he knew her more than Tammy knew about. Rico had been good to her. She hadn't had a reason to doubt him. More than likely, she still didn't have a reason to doubt him. Something just didn't seem right to her about this. She didn't want to start an argument, so she kept her thoughts to herself. Finally, Tammy replied to Rico, "No, baby, that is fine. I am sure that someone is there with her. If not, Cashmere will be there soon. Thank you for offering, though. That is so sweet of you, baby!" She threw that last part in to ensure he wasn't worried about her answer. Since she had taken a few minutes to respond.

Rico wondered if she was a little jealous about his text. He didn't let on that it was of any concern to him. "Okay, baby. Keep me posted, though." Their text fell silent for a few moments, and then Tammy finally sent her reply, "Okay, baby, I will." As quick as their text had started, they ended even quicker. There wasn't any "I love you, or I miss you," like usual. Tammy knew that something wasn't right. She also knew that he knew that something wasn't right. Until now, things had been great between them. Now, something loomed over the top of their relationship.

Rico looked at her last few texts and knew something wasn't right with her. He wondered what she was thinking. Could this be something that would rock their relationship? Was there something happening on the ship she wasn't telling him about? His mind wandered to the worst that could happen. Has she met someone else already? Was their relationship too weak to withstand this time apart? His mind roamed to places he didn't want it to venture towards. He then put his thoughts aside. Knowing what he had in Tammy, he would cross that bridge when he had to. Deep down inside, he hoped it would never happen. He took a drive to ease his mind. He ended up at The Crib. R.J. was there doing inventory for their weekly order. Rico poured himself an ice cold beer and helped R.J. As much as he tried, he couldn't get his mind off Tammy. He knew something concerned her about Ingrid, but he couldn't help but wonder if his offer struck her the wrong way. He wanted to call her and talk to her about it, but he wasn't sure if it was wise.

Tammy was thinking about what he had said, too. She kept wondering if there was something more. Finally, she decided she would try to put it out of her mind until something more became of it. Stephanie said, "Girl, let's get out of this room and see what's happening on the ship." Those were the words that Tammy needed to hear. So they both set out to see what was going on. Stephanie decided she needed something to eat, so they went to one restaurant to grab a bite. While eating, Stephanie could see that Tammy had something on her mind. She told Tammy, "Look, either call him and find out what is going on or deal with this after the trip. We will not enjoy our vacation until you get past this or handle it. One or the other, but please decide." "I know it is probably nothing. I am probably overthinking it." "You know, you have always had a tough time picking the right men. Maybe that is bothering you. Rico is a good man! Sometimes he seems too good to be true, but that is not a reason to doubt him." Stephanie said. "Girl, I know, you may be right. Deep down, I sincerely hope you are. I am truly in love with him. I really think he is the one!"

Tammy's phone chirped again… she picked it up, hoping it was Rico again. But instead, it was Cashmere, saying she had made it to the hospital. She was with Ingrid, and things weren't going so well. The doctor was trying to stop the labor, but if they couldn't, they would have to do a c-section. The chances of the baby surviving were dismal. Tammy let Stephanie read the text; tears overcame both of them. This was indeed a sad occasion. If Ingrid lost the baby, it would be hard for them to overcome this. They were all like family. Ingrid was like their little sister.

Surprised by Ingrid's pregnancy in the first place, they had grown accustomed to the thought of being aunts to her baby. They had already planned a baby shower when they returned. Just when it seemed everything was going well for them. This had to happen. She replied to Cashmere's text, letting her know they would keep them in their prayers and they wished for the best. Her words seemed as if they weren't enough for this, but it was all she could muster for now. Anything more, and she would probably cry. She knew tears would eventually come, but she wasn't ready for them now. She needed to concentrate on making this trip the best it could be. Just her and Stephanie were left, so they had to make the best of it.

The sun had set on the ocean, and the stars were more visible. There was a nice ocean breeze flowing throughout the ship. Stephanie and Tammy had returned to the room to get ready to go to "Flawless," one of the ship's nite clubs. When they arrived at the club, it was very crowded. There is a table in the far left corner of the stage. They sat down, and a waiter came over and said, "Tammy and Stephanie, I presume." They both looked at him with a look of uncertainty. "Yes," Stephanie answered. "I am Trent, the head waiter here on the Diamond Line." "Trent, how did you know who we were?" Tammy asked. "Sorry, I should have stated that before. We got a call from Rico; he stated that there was someone special to him on this cruise and that we should make sure they want for nothing, so he asked us to bill him for all your drinks for the entire cruise. He also asked us to ensure you had the best tables in all the nightclubs and restaurants." Stephanie looked at Tammy, and they both smiled. Trent waved to one of the crew members; he brought over a vase filled with a dozen red roses. Another waiter came to the table with a plate of chocolate-covered strawberries and a giant bottle of Moscato. "Rico said we should start the evening off with these treats. I hope everything is in order. Please enjoy; we will be back shortly to see if there is anything else that you require."

Trent stated. "Thank you so much!" Tammy said. "Oh, don't thank me. Thank Rico! He made this happen. One of you must be special to him. I would say one of you is very lucky to have someone go out of their way like this for you!" Trent stated. He smiled and walked away. Stephanie looked at Tammy and said, "Damn, girl, that man loves the ground you walk on. You are lucky to have someone to care that much for you!" "Yeah, I guess I am. This is more than nice of him. He is fantastic!" "I would say so." Stephanie agreed. Tammy looked at the flowers and noticed a card. When she read the card, her eyes teared up. The card read: "Tammy, I am missing you; more than one man could miss anyone! I hope these roses bring a smile to your face. I yearn to see your smile again, with eternal love, Rico!" With that, Tammy poured her and Stephanie a glass of Moscato.

Chapter 3

It was three in the morning in Italy, and Char was just returning to her hotel room after a long day of posing for her photoshoot. She arrived in Italy two days ago. It was right around the time that her girls were about to set sail. Char wanted to be there with them, but work seemed to be never-ending these days. She had never been to Italy before, so she didn't want to miss out on this either. Although Italy was everything she had expected, she still missed her girls.

Char took a shower to wash the workday off of her. She poured herself a small glass of wine before she went to bed. As hard as she tried to fall asleep, something was not letting her do so. She tossed and turned until about five am. Finally, she called Tammy to see how things were going.

Char… Hey girl, how is the trip going?

Tammy… it could be better.

Char… Why? What happened?

Tammy… Have you talked to Cashmere at all?

Char… No, I haven't. What's going on, Tammy?

Tammy… Ingrid is in the hospital. She's in labor, and the baby is not doing so well.

Char… Oh no, Tammy. Where is Cashmere? May I speak to her?

Tammy… Cashmere is back in Virginia. She went to be with Ingrid to make sure she was okay.

Char… This is crazy. I thought Ingrid was doing well. How did this happen?

Tammy… Apparently, they found out the baby was breech, and then suddenly, she went into labor.

Char… There are plenty of babies that have been born breech. There must be something more that she isn't saying.

Tammy… You may be right. Cashmere will find out, though. I will call you when I know more.

Char… All right, that sounds good. I need to get to sleep, anyway. I have to prepare for a photo shoot at eleven. My eyes will be so puffy in the morning.

Tammy… Wow, the life of a model. Okay, I will keep you posted about Ingrid. Good night Char.

Char… Good night.

They both hung up the phone. Char looked at the clock. It was now six in the morning, and she was still awake. Now it was even harder for her to fall asleep. She had to be on the set in five hours, meaning she had about three or four hours to sleep. Not only would her eyes be puffy, but she would be very sleepy. It was around six forty-five when she finally drifted off to sleep. Her alarm went off at nine-thirty in the morning. Char was not in the best of moods this morning. She was always cranky when she didn't get enough sleep, which was more often than not. She hoped she cursed nobody out today. At about ten thirty, her driver arrived to take her to the photo shoot. Quickly jumped in the car before anybody noticed her. She grabbed an energy drink from the limo refrigerator. She knew she would need this one and another to get her through the long day ahead. When she arrived at the shoot, the energy drink had kicked in. She went by the food table; put grapes and strawberries on a plate. Picked up a glass of orange juice and headed to the make-up room. When she got to the make-up room, two other models were already having their make-up applied. She sat in one chair and ate her fruit while waiting for her make-up artist to enter the room. She overheard the two other make-up artists saying that the other artist would be late. That would push Char's whole day back. She needed to be on the set at two pm. She wasn't certain she would be there on time. Hopefully, the artist would get there soon, or another would finish soon. Char continued eating her fruit when another make-up artist walked in. He was tall, bald, and thin, looking right at her. He walked to the other make-up artist to speak with them for a minute. She could barely hear what they were saying because they seemed to whisper to one another. She hoped they were talking about him doing her hair. Then she heard him say, "Hello… my name is Antonio, and I will be your cosmetic technician today." "Hello Antonio, I am Char. It's very nice to meet you!" Char said with a smile. "It is very nice to meet you as well! I have seen your work, and you are gorgeous!" As he smiled, showing his perfect white teeth. She wondered if he was flirting with her. "Thank you!" She said as she smiled back at him. He pulled her hair back and asked her, "What look are we going for today?" "Well, it is supposed to be a seductive and sassy look." "Seductive and sassy, I can definitely do that. I won't need to apply much make-up to you for that. You have the seductive part down already." Now she was certain he was flirting with her. She found this interesting, so she thought she would see just how interesting this could get. "Well, that is very nice of you to say, Antonio. Not sure how true it is, but nice!" Again, she gave him a smile. He smiled back. "It is true! In my line of work, I see a lot of beautiful women, so I know exactly what I am talking about." "Well, Antonio, I appreciate your words." He applied her make-up. He was very meticulous in his application. After he was done, he asked: "May I take a selfie with you?" "Do you normally take selfies with your clients?" "Well, to be honest, no, but you are not a normal client of mine." "And why is that?" "Well, you are one I want to see again. If I have a selfie of you, I can see you whenever I want!" "I don't mind, but I prefer it when my hair is done." "You're lucky then because I will also do your hair." "You do hair as well?" "Yes, I am a hairstylist." "Well, how are you going to do my hair?" "In my professional opinion, I think we should pull it back, have it flowing down your back, with a nice wet look." "Oh, that sounds nice. I wanted nothing too elaborate. Do you think the camera will like it?" "Most definitely. I know I will like it. Great, let's get started then." Antonio worked his magic once again. She enjoyed the feeling of his hands in her hair. When he was done, he spun her around so she could see herself in the mirror. It amazed her at the look he gave her. "So, how about that selfie?" He asked. She smiled and nodded her head up and down. He smiled back at her, took the pic, and asked would you like me to send it to you?" "Antonio, are you asking me for my phone number?" "Yes, I am." "I see you are not only beautiful but clever. Yes, I am asking you for your phone number." "Nicely done, Antonio, nicely done. You may have my number. I hope you do more with it than just send a pic of us." "Please don't worry; I will do more with it!" They both smiled. He saved her number to his phone and sent her the pic. Just as she was saving his number, the photographer's assistant came and said: "Char, the photographer is ready for you now." "I will be right there. Thank you, Antonio It was truly a pleasure meeting you. I hope to hear from you soon." She got up, smiled, and walked away. Antonio watched her walk to the door... "Char... it was very nice meeting you, too." She turned to look at him, smiled again, and walked out. Antonio liked what he saw in Char. He knew he would call her soon.

Chapter 4

Still enjoying the beautiful surprise that Rico had given them, the girls were finally trying to enjoy their vacation. Although it wasn't the same without Cashmere, they were still trying to make the best of the trip. Tammy was pouring another round of Moscato for her and Stephanie. Lights dimmed, and a man walked out; he announced a band would perform shortly. The next thing they knew, a Jackson 5 tribute band was taking the stage. They started with "ABC" and then rolled into "Rockin Robin." By the time they started the second song, they had packed the dance floor. Tammy and Stephanie were out there getting their groove on. This music was great. Captured so much of their originality and showmanship. I really enjoyed seeing the Jackson 5 tribute band perform. They loved every song that the band performed. They laughed and danced until their feet were sore. Stephanie and Tammy finally felt like they were on vacation; this was what the good life was all about. Rico had really made them feel special. Tammy felt better about what had happened between them. She may have been feeding too much into this. Rico was a good man. She also knew that Rico was the one for her. Not just because he surprised her with all the goodies, but because it was felt deep within her heart. He was everything she needed to complete her. She hadn't felt this way for anyone in a very long time. In fact, she didn't expect to feel this way for another man. She had been okay with just doing her. She is getting her life together, achieving all she can reach. She was good without a man in her life but feeling blessed, he came into her life. At this point in her life, she realized you can't rush love from the right person. Instead, wait for true love to find you. True love has found her this time. Stephanie looked at Tammy and asked, "Girl, where are your thoughts?" "I'm sorry; I was thinking about Rico and how happy I am with him!" "Girl, you have plenty of time to think about Rico. We are on vacation, and it is time to enjoy sisterhood!" "I hear you." They laughed, clinked their wine glasses, and took another sip. This cruise was everything they needed to get their minds off the insanities of their lives.

Stephanie had been smiling and laughing since they had been in the club. This trip was everything she had expected so far. They didn't have to worry about anything; Stephanie had thought about her restaurant. The restaurant manager had called her twice already. She finally had to tell him he was the manager for a reason. She also told him not to call unless it was an emergency. When she looked up, Tammy was smiling from ear to ear. Tammy was having just as good of a time as she was having.

Rico had taken great care of them. Tammy had planned to thank him properly when she saw him again. Missing him right now. She wanted to be in his arms. Her thoughts had gravitated to making love with him. Then she heard Stephanie's voice coming into her thoughts. "Hello Tammy, are you still here? Come back from wherever you are!" She felt something touch her hand, her eyes focused on Stephanie's hand moving away from her hand. "Tammy, were you thinking about your man again?" "Girl, look, he is everything. I can't help but think about him! He thrills me!" "Um, okay. Remember, we are on vacation. We should have fun." Oh, my bad. Did you not have fun with all the goodies Rico provided for us?" "I appreciate all that he has done. I don't want you to think about him so much that you forget why we are here." "Oh, I see now. You didn't have a problem enjoying all the perks earlier tonight. You were all over the chocolate-covered strawberries, the drinks, and everything else he provided. You had nothing to say then. Now suddenly, I should not think about him and pay all my attention to you." "That's not what I am saying. I enjoyed all the VIP treatment he provided for us. I want you to take full advantage of this vacation. We have been planning this for a very long time. Cashmere is already gone; it's just you and I here now. I'm just saying, let's really enjoy this vacation." "I hear what you are saying. I don't know how much we can enjoy this vacation without everyone being with us. And speaking of Cashmere, we should try to call her. We need to check on Ingrid." "I want to call, but I am not sure how things are going, and I don't want to make matters worse." "Tammy, I understand what you mean. I am sure if things get bad, Cashmere will call and let us know." "You may be right, Stephanie. Let's call her tomorrow and see how things are going."

The ship would dock in Miami tomorrow before it set out for Bermuda. A half day of shopping, eating, and just enjoying being anywhere but home is just what these two friends need. When they woke up the following day, excitement filled the room. They were about to hang out in Miami for a few hours. Stephanie wanted to try the city's great food, while Tammy wanted to do sightseeing. They both wanted to get some shopping done before they boarded to leave. Once they got off the ship, they walked around the boardwalk just to see what it offered. There were lots of little novelty shops, restaurants and lots of people. They walked past this one restaurant, and Stephanie immediately stopped in her tracks.

"Are you okay, Stephanie?" Tammy asked. "Yes, I am fine. Don't you smell that?" "Smell what?" "That wonderful aroma!" Stephanie turned her head in the smell's direction and noticed a crowd of people already inside. "Come on," Stephanie said. She grabbed Tammy's hand and pulled her into the restaurant. They walked up to the counter and were greeted by the waitress. "Hello... welcome to A Taste Of The Sea. How may I help you?" Tammy looked at Stephanie and said, "How may she help us, Stephanie?" Stephanie replied, "What is that mesmerizing smell?" The waitress smiled and said, "That is our special of the day, baked Alaskan cod."

"May I please have an order of that"? Stephanie asked. The waitress looked at Tammy and asked: "And for you, ma'am?" "I guess I will have the same as my girlfriend." They both walked over to a little corner table overlooking the ocean. Tammy looked at Stephanie and just laughed. "What's so funny?" Stephanie asked. "You are what's so funny. Once a chef, always a chef!" "Didn't that smell divine to you?" Stephanie asked. "I guess it smelled okay," Tammy replied. "I think it will surprise you when you receive the meal. It will be well worth our time if it tastes half as good as it smells." When the dish arrived, it was wrapped in banana leaves. Tammy and Stephanie opened their leaves, and the aroma of greatness filled their nostrils with nothing but goodness. Stephanie cut into her baked Alaskan cod, and the fish fell apart. From her first taste, the flavors layered their savoriness throughout every bite. Stephanie was in her heaven. She wanted to savor every bit of this wonderfulness.

Meanwhile, Tammy wasn't as impressed. She thought it was regular ole fish wrapped in some want-to-be unique leaves. Stephanie knew Tammy wouldn't enjoy it as much as her but wanted her to experience the meal just the same. She hoped Tammy would grasp how the flavors married one another to make the dish a more enjoyable experience.

After finishing their meal, they continued to walk the boardwalk. Tables lined the pathway where people were selling many items from Miami. Tammy noticed a colorful table displaying a vast array of seashells; seashells were one of Ingrid's favorite items. She had been collecting since she was a little girl. They stopped at the table to see what they offered. The seashell she found was a dark brown color with blue speckles in the top portion. She knew Ingrid would just love it. She quickly purchased the seashell, and a tear eased down her eye because her thoughts went to Ingrid and what she was dealing with at this very moment. Although Tammy didn't really know the gravity of the situation, fearing it wouldn't be good... She felt that the gift would bring a smile to Ingrid's face. She hoped that this would ease the pain she was going through. If it could help just a little, it would be worth it.

Stephanie walked down the boardwalk and found a gift for Ingrid. She saw a plaque: "When our fears are at an all-time high, that's when our strength will need to persevere!" She thought this plaque would bring hope. Some extra fortitude for her and everything she was going through. Stephanie and Tammy wished they could be there with Ingrid and the family. They knew they would be there as soon as they returned to Virginia. Cashmere would need the support.

Chapter 5

Back in Virginia, Cashmere was with Ingrid. Her contractions were getting closer and closer. Cashmere was trying to keep Ingrid calm, but she was having difficulty doing so. The baby was trying to come into this world. The situation was getting worse. Ingrid was not responding to the terbutaline they had given her to stop the labor. This baby was not taking "no" for an answer! Cashmere could see that Ingrid was exhausted and needed rest. Unfortunately, she had a long way to go before she could rest. The pain of her labor showed on her face. It was easily the most trying experience that Ingrid had gone through in her life. She looked over at Cashmere, parted her lips, and in between contractions, uttered the words, "I am glad you're here!" Cashmere reached for Ingrid's hand, wrapped her fingers around it, and said: "Me too!" Just then, Cashmere thought back to when they were kids, and Ingrid was always trying to be by her side.

The two of them fought like enemies sometimes. Other times, they were the best of friends. Now she looked over at her baby sister and saw she would bring a life into the world soon. She was doing something Cashmere had often thought about but hadn't done yet. Although this pregnancy was far from planned, she still accomplished something Cashmere had always dreamed about doing. She looked at her little sister with overwhelming envy in her eyes. While Ingrid lay there trying to muster all the energy she had to keep from pushing, this baby was determined to make its presence known. The terbutaline was not working. The contractions were still coming. They were getting stronger and stronger. The nurse came into the room to check on Ingrid. Cashmere immediately said, "She needs more drugs. The contractions are still coming!" The nurse reviewed the progression of her contraction by looking at the monitor. She saw Cashmere was right. She also knew that Ingrid was not due for more medications for another twenty minutes. Both the nurse and Cashmere looked at Ingrid, wondering the same thing. Could Ingrid hold out another twenty minutes? The pain on her face had increased to agony. Ingrid tried to bear it, but her face bore the truth! It was turning out to be real bad, real quick. Suddenly, Cashmere saw her baby sister suffering, and she knew she couldn't do anything to help her. She squeezed Ingrid's hand harder and said, "It will be all right. I am here for you! We will get through this together!" Ingrid looked over at Cashmere, tears in her eyes. She tried to speak, but the pain was too great for her to make a sound. Ingrid was scared. She was unsure about what would happen next. All she knew was that she needed this to be over. She needed this baby to come so that the pain would cease! Finally, the nurse said, "We can give her more medicine now." She added the terbutaline to the intravenous bag. They all hoped that it would stop her labor soon. The nurse knew the medicine would take at least fifteen minutes either way. The concern was that this was her third dose of terbutaline, and she seemed to be immune to the effects of the medication. She could not have any more until tomorrow. So, if this one didn't work, Ingrid could not have any more tonight. She would have to wait until the next day. This labor was the most unpleasant event in any of their lives, especially Ingrid's. Cashmere needed air. She needed to take a quick walk, but something scared her to leave Ingrid. The nurse looked at her face and said: "If you need to go to the gift shop or the restroom, I will be here for at least another ten minutes." The nurse had read Cashmere's face. "Yes, I need to go to the restroom for a minute." Cashmere got up to walk out, turned to the nurse, and mouthed, "Thank you!" The nurse nodded her head as Cashmere turned to walk out the door. Once, she exited the room and turned the corner. Tears flowed. She didn't know what was going on, but she knew that this labor was not going well, and it should be. She knew something was wrong. Something that neither the nurses nor the doctors were speaking about yet. It pained her to think her sister was suffering horribly and that she wasn't out of the woods yet! She needed someone to talk to about this; she knew she needed to talk to her girls! She also knew that time would not permit it right now. She had to return to Ingrid to ensure she was okay or not getting any worse. She already felt guilty about being away from her. She was walking back to the hospital room, and right before she entered, she saw Uncle Herbert turn the corner. "Cashmere!" He said. "How is she?" She stopped and turned in his direction. He looked into her eyes, and they instantly walked toward one another! She fell into his arms. "Uncle Herbert, she is having a tough time! I don't know what's happening, but something is wrong." "What is the doctor saying, baby?" "That's just it, Uncle Herbert. They have said nothing yet. They keep giving her medication, which she needs. They aren't talking. It seems they aren't sure what to say or when to say it." "Okay, baby, we will find out what is going on with her." "Uncle Herbert, I am so glad you are here!" "Me too, baby, me too! Remind me; we have something we need to talk about when this is over." Cashmere looked at her uncle, thought for a few seconds, and said: "Okay, I will remind you, Uncle Herbert." She looked into her uncle's eyes, and he returned the look. Trying to figure out what was on his mind. In her heart, she already knew what was on his mind. "Come on, Cash, let's go check on Ingrid." She hadn't heard him call her that since she was a little girl. She had missed him calling her that. It brought back splendid memories of when they would spend time together. He was her favorite uncle at one point. She wondered why he was calling her that, suddenly. She didn't let him know she was curious about why he said it tonight. She was sure he was aware, though. Instead, she played along and said: "Come on, Uncle Herbie; let's go see how Ingrid is doing."

When they walked into the room, they saw the nurse and the doctor looking at the monitor and talking amongst themselves. They both looked at Ingrid, who appeared to be in more pain. Tears were flowing down her face. Cashmere knew that Ingrid couldn't hold them back now. The pain must have been more intense. Then things heated; Uncle Herbert shouted, "What's going on here? Tell me what the hell is happening with my niece." Hearing the directness in his voice, the doctor looked up and said: "Hello, sir, I am Dr. Bland, and I am the physician assigned to this patient."

"It's nice to meet you, Dr. Bland; can you please tell me what is going on? She looks so uncomfortable." "Well, sir, she is in preterm labor. We have been trying to stop the contractions by giving her terbutaline. The terbutaline is not taking. We may have one more chance in the early morning. We will have to let the baby come if it does not take." "Doctor, you don't sound too sure about letting the baby come. What are we talking about?" "Sir, in all honesty, I am uncertain that this is the best approach. If we do this, we could have serious complications with the patient and the baby. Ingrid should have another two weeks of pregnancy before it would be safe for her to give birth." "Is there anything else that can be done to prevent this birth?" "Unfortunately, sir, this is the last option. She can't stay in labor for two more weeks. If the terbutaline does not take this afternoon, we will have no choice but to prepare her for surgery." "What are the chances she and the baby will be okay?" "Sir, please understand we will do everything we can to ensure the safety." "Don't give me the disclaimer. I want the truth. What are their chances of surviving this labor?" "Sir, the baby has about fifty percent chances of living, although it might challenge her mental capacity." "What are Ingrid's chances of survival?" "Well, we have found that Ingrid has a heart condition, and this labor could strain her heart too much to make it." "Man, what are you saying?" "Sir, I am saying Ingrid may not make it through this labor. There is a ninety percent chance that her heart will fail in labor." "Then there is a ten percent chance that her heart will make it through this." "Yes, there is that chance." "Then that is what we will go with then; we will focus on the positive rather than the negative." "Please believe we will do everything we can to care for her and the baby!"

Uncle Herbert looked over at Cashmere and Ingrid; they both had tears. Uncle Herbert went over to Ingrid, reached for her hand, then the three of them hugged. "We'll get through this as a family. Everything will be fine." Uncle Herbert said. It was far too much for any of them to handle. At this point, they all seemed to realize just how serious this was becoming. Ingrid knew she had a long road ahead of her. She was about to face her most formidable challenge in life. Ingrid knew that giving birth to this child could mean the end of her life. Yet, she found enough strength to smile at the fact she would be a mother soon. It would be magical no matter how long motherhood would last for her! Her thoughts went to hoping that she would live long enough to see her child at least, maybe hold her. She knew they would care for her child. Cashmere and Uncle Herbert would make sure of that.

Chapter 6

After another long day of photos and clothing changes, Char was finally on her way back to the hotel for some much-needed rest. When she exited the limo, her phone rang.

Char... Hello

Antonio... Hello Char, this is Antonio

Char... Antonio, and how are you?

Antonio... I am well, thanks. I wanted to call and say it was a pleasure meeting you today.

Char... Thank you very much. It was a pleasure to meet you as well.

Antonio... How did your shoot go?

Char... It went well.

Antonio... And your hair and makeup... did they hold up for you?

Char... Yes, they did... I think I owe it all to the most outstanding cosmetic technician in the world.

Antonio... Oh, you are sweet... So what is it you owe?

Char... Well, what exactly are you asking?

Antonio... I am asking if I can see you again.

Char... Well, what do you have in mind?

Antonio... I was thinking about dinner.

Char... Dinner sounds interesting.

Antonio... Great, how about tomorrow evening?

Char... Tomorrow evening sounds excellent... How about around 7?

Antonio... That sounds great... I will pick you up at 7.

Char... Okay, I will text you the address of my hotel.

Antonio... Great, see you tomorrow, Char.

When Char ended the call, she couldn't help but crack a smile. She thought Antonio was a nice enough person. She liked how he spoke with her while making her look glamorous. He had piqued her interest. His call had added to that pique. She hoped that their date would heighten her interest even more. When Char got to her room, her smile hadn't left her face. She saved Antonio as a contact and sent him the hotel address. He responded, "thank you."

Char grabbed a bottle of Moscato from the refrigerator and some strawberries. She went to the bathroom, ran bath water, and poured a bubble bath in the tub. She eased into the tub with her glass of wine and a bowl of strawberries and relaxed. Her mind quickly wandered from Antonio to Ingrid and her girls. She knew she had to call them soon. She was hesitant because she wasn't sure how bad the news would be. She concentrated on relaxing and enjoying her bath. She would deal with the call later. For now, she would just lay back and let the soothing bubbles calm her body while the Moscato would relax her even more. Before too long, Char was settled.

The strawberries were gone, and her glass of Moscato was empty. The bubbles had all but disappeared from the tub. She toweled dry, lotioned her body, slipped on her nightgown, and prepared to just relax. Her day had been long and hard. Meeting Antonio made it better, but she was tired. The life of a model could be very demanding. Most of the time, it did little for her social life. Her thoughts moved toward Antonio and how nice he seemed to be. She knew it was only a few days before she would return home. There would not be much time for her to get to know him. These are the moments when it's hard to be a world-famous model. It was a part of her life she knew would not get any easier. She knew that sometimes you have to take the good with the bad. She was fortunate to be in a career she loved. However, she was unfortunate not to have a love to share it all with. She had often contemplated giving it all up and finding her true love. She knew she would probably go crazy without modeling. She enjoyed the travel, the lifestyle, and the glamour way too much to walk away from it all. Besides, she knew the life of a model didn't last that long. She figured she had plenty of time after modeling to find her true love. Deep down, she knew she was a career woman who had put love on the back burner. Like her girls, they all had lost their way with love and relationships with men. Although, now, two of them may have found their way back to love. Char was envious of Tammy. She wanted what she had with Rico, yet she wasn't willing to give up her career for it. She knew she had a meaningful life, but romantically, it was a lonely life. It was a life of travel, hotels, and meeting many people. Although she didn't really have time to get to know those people. Still, it was enough for her right now.

Chapter 7

It was early morning, and the ocean breeze flowed into the porthole just as Tammy opened her eyes. Stephanie had already been up and was in the bathroom, brushing her teeth. She planned to go down for breakfast and lounge in the chair to breathe the fresh ocean air. Maybe see some dolphins or whales while she relaxes. Tammy got up and walked towards the bathroom, scratching her head. "Damn girl, I forgot how rough you look in the morning! Has Rico seen you in the morning?" "Of course, he has seen me in the morning! Girl, he loves me just the way I am." "Did he tell you that?" "No, but I know he does. He doesn't have to tell me that." "Yeah, okay. You are going to scare him away, looking like that!" "You have your nerve, Stephanie. You're not a runway model yourself in the morning!" Girl, I may not be a runway model, but you are not a curb model." "Okay, now you are going too far. You better stop, or I may have to cut you." "Cut me? Girl, you are crazy!" There was a knock at the door. When Tammy opened it, flowers and a card were sitting on the floor. When Stephanie saw them, she immediately said, "Damn, that brother Rico loves you. First, the VIP status on the cruise now flowers. You got a good one, girl; you better keep him!" Tammy started smiling. She thought they were from Rico, then she looked at the name on the card, which read "Stephanie." "Umm, no, girl. They aren't for me. They are for you!" Stephanie had a clueless look on her face. She didn't think that anybody would send her flowers. She read the card, "I can't wait until we have our dinner together." Stephanie tried to hold back her smile, but she couldn't. Her smile was radiant and contagious because Tammy couldn't help but smile. "You have someone's attention." "I do, and I am not sure I like his attention." Tammy looks at Stephanie with concern. She wasn't exactly sure what she meant by that. Tammy had to ask, "What do you mean? Is there something creepy about him?" "Well, I haven't quite figured him out yet. He seems interested, but I am just not sure about him." She didn't have a reason not to like him. He had done nothing to give her an uneasy feeling. Yet she just wasn't sure about Detective Cruz. "Are you going to have dinner with him?" Tammy asked. "I think so. I am not sure yet. I am inquisitive about him," Stephanie replied. "Well, hopefully, the dinner date goes well," Tammy said. She knew Stephanie was going to have dinner with him. She was probably going to fall for him, too. She just didn't want to admit it right now. Tammy knew Stephanie liked the back of her hand. Stephanie fell in love quickly when there was someone to fall in love with. When she wasn't consumed with her career, which was never what she had focused on for the last couple of years. Stephanie always puts her all into her relationships, which is what you are supposed to do. Unfortunately, most of the guys she dated were only attracted to her parent's money. Although Stephanie was clueless about that until a few years back. There was Jeremiah, whom she thought was the love of her life. She gave him everything. She did everything for him, and he did nothing for her. He took her love and manipulated her into giving him whatever he wanted. That relationship lasted almost a year, but she never could truly get over him. She sort of walked away from being in a committed relationship after him. That's when she turned her focus toward her career. She changed, and the Stephanie that we now know and love emerged. So, that's why Stephanie is uncertain about Detective Cruz because she is uncertain that she wants to go down that road again. It was too painful an experience the last time. We all know that love is part of life. A part of life that is very important to most of us. We all say that we don't need love or a significant other in our lives, but the truth is that we would rather have love in our lives than not! Stephanie had been without real love for a while now. She had a flourishing career but no one to share it all with. That made for a lonely life. She knew it was time to let someone in, but she was too scared to go through it again. She would need a great man to come along, someone she could trust. Someone she knew would love her for more than her or her parent's money. Could Detective Cruz be that guy? Would he love her unconditionally? Would he be the one that would stay by her side when she needed him most? Those were the questions that she needed answers to. The questions that meant the most to her. The questions that the other men had faltered with before him. It would appear that Detective Cruz had a lot to prove. The only thing was that he had no clue about the mountain he had to climb just to gain Stephanie's attention. Tammy knew that any man interested in Stephanie had a long hard road ahead. She felt sorry for Detective Cruz because he may be a nice man, but by the time Stephanie was done with him, he might have some regrets about pursuing her. That is such a shame because Stephanie deserves true love. She has just been scorned so badly that she doesn't know how to trust a man anymore. Although he didn't know it, Detective Cruz had much to prove, and Stephanie had much to be cautious of. This was not a recipe for a long-lasting relationship. They hadn't even had dinner yet, and it stacked the cards against them. Unfortunately for Stephanie, the cards were stacked against any man that showed interest in her. Her trust wasn't something that she would easily give away anymore. Especially after the ordeal with Matthius trying to chloroform her. She still didn't know what was up with that. Who knew his intentions if he had actually gotten away with it? The only thing she knew about Detective Cruz was that she could feel safe around him. She knew he wouldn't let harm come her way. Still, she couldn't truly let her guard down with him. He had to prove himself first. And little did he know, prove himself, he would certainly do. If he wanted her attention! Tammy and Stephanie had spent a couple of hours discussing all of this. They were dressed but hadn't left the stateroom yet. By the time they had gotten to the Lido deck, breakfast was almost over. They saw Captain Henderson walking by. He stopped and asked how they were doing. Captain Henderson also asked about Cashmere. After they told him how things were going for Cashmere, he asked if they had enough to eat. He told them he would ensure they got their fill since they arrived at the end of breakfast. He motioned for a waiter and told the waiter to get them whatever they wanted. Tammy and Stephanie ordered a few items, the waiter took off, and within about fifteen minutes, he was back with their meals. He had also brought them fruit and juices to enjoy. Tammy took out her phone, looked up Cashmere's number, and called her. It was about time for them to know exactly what was going on with Ingrid. Cashmere answered the phone. Tammy could tell that she was a little groggy. She must have been asleep. "I'm sorry if I woke you. I just wanted to check on you and Ingrid," Tammy said. "It's all good, girl; I was just getting a little rest. I am here with Ingrid. She is having a rough time." "What's going on with her Cashmere?" "Well, the baby is a breach; Ingrid is in premature labor. The doctors are trying to stop the labor, but the medicine isn't working. To top it all off, Ingrid has a heart condition. They say her chances of making it through the delivery are slim." Tammy had put the phone on speaker so Stephanie could hear too. "I am so sorry to hear all of this, Cashmere. Please give Ingrid our best." Stephanie said. Tammy was speechless. She couldn't believe what she had just heard. All of them were fighting off tears. This was truly a sad situation. It really wasn't what Tammy and Stephanie were expecting to hear. They knew the situation was serious but didn't know it was death-defying. Ingrid was way too young to be in this predicament.

Chapter 8

"Cashmere," Ingrid uttered. "Yes, Ingrid." "If I don't get through this, please take care of my baby. I want her name to be Ingrid Cashmere Riggins." "Ingrid, don't talk like that. You will make it through this." "I hope I will, but if I don't, I need to know someone will take her. I want nobody else to do it but you!" "I promise you, Ingrid, I will take good care of her if you don't make it through this. I know you will, though! I know you will!" Another contraction came, and Ingrid grimaced with pain. The pain was increasing with every contraction she had. It was becoming unbearable. Cashmere knew that her little sister couldn't take much more of this pain. She also knew the doctors couldn't do much more for her. They were trying to make her as comfortable as they could. Suddenly, the door swung open, and a voice shouted, "Ingrid!" They all looked towards the door; Ingrid smiled and screamed, "D!" Cashmere took one look at "D" and shouted, "Hell no, Damion!" Damion said, "Cashmere, what are you doing here?" "What am I doing here? What the hell are you doing here?" "Ingrid is my girl. She is pregnant with my baby. That's what I am doing here." "How do you know "D," Cashmere?" Ingrid asked. "Damion and I dated in middle school for two weeks. No, Ingrid, this can't be happening. You can't be pregnant by him." "You are Ingrid's sister? Isn't this a small world?" Damion said. Cashmere shot him a look that said I could kill you right now. "What is this true "D"?" Ingrid questioned. "Yes, Ingrid, we dated in middle school. I didn't know that you were her sister, though!" "Oh God, please don't let this happen. Please don't let this be the truth!" Uncle Herbert stated. Ingrid let out a scream of agony. Another contraction was setting in. They seemed to come more frequently and lasted longer. The nurse went to get the doctor. "Ingrid, are you okay, baby?" "D," asked. "No, fool. She is not okay. This baby is coming, and the chances of both of them making it through this delivery are slim." Cashmere said with anger. "Stop arguing. I need you two to get along! This baby is coming, and I need to get things straight before it comes. Cashmere and "D," if I don't make it out of this alive. I want you both to raise the baby." Ingrid said. "What? What do you mean, sweetie?" "D," he said. "I mean just that, "D." I want you and my sister to raise this baby together. Promise me you will both raise this baby!" Ingrid stated matter-of-factly. "I'm not sure about that, Ingrid. You know I would do anything for you, but I am not sure the two of us raising this baby will work." Cashmere said. "If you would do anything for me, then do this. Don't think about it; just do it!" Ingrid demanded. "Baby, I am the father of this baby. I don't need her help to raise our baby. And stop talking like you will not make it through this." "D," she said. "Fool, haven't you been listening? Don't you see what's happening here? This is a dangerous situation! I finally know my purpose now. It was meant for me to bring this child into the world. I will fulfill my destiny. I need the two of you to take care of everything else! Promise me you both will raise this baby. Promise me!" Ingrid said. "I have to think about that, Ingrid. I can't make that decision right now." Cashmere replied. "Cashmere, unfortunately, make that decision now. I need to know before this baby comes. I am not guaranteed to make it through this." Ingrid said, trying to hold back the tears running down her face. Uncle Herbert looked at Cashmere and Damion and said: "What are y'all going to do?" Silence fell over the room for what seemed like an eternity. The doctor came into the room to check Ingrid's cervix. "Ingrid, you are dilated to ten centimeters. This baby will be here soon. There is nothing else we can do. We have to move forward with the delivery. Nurse, please have the tech set up delivery room four stat!" "If that is your wish, Ingrid, I will abide by it." stated "D." They all looked at Cashmere, awaiting her answer. "Cashmere!!!!!" shouted Uncle Herbert. Cashmere looked around the room before walking to the window to hide the tears in her eyes. Looking out the window, she knew this was a huge decision. She also knew this was possibly the last time her sister would ask her anything. If she did this, she would have to deal with Damion for the rest of her life. If she said no, she would hurt her sister. The clock was ticking. She knew she had to decide. "Cashmere, I know things didn't go well between us. I also know that you probably hate me, too. We must put our differences behind us and do what's right for Ingrid and the baby!" Damion said. Cashmere turned around and looked at Damion. "You are right; I hate you! I will do this for my sister, though. I am telling you, if you don't hold up to your end of the deal, I will take your ass to court and take this baby from you. Do you understand me?" Cashmere said. Ingrid smiled, but her smile was short-lived because another contraction had forced its way through. "God, please help me through this!" Ingrid said while trying to deal with the pain. This was the hardest thing she had ever dealt with. Faced with the fact she might not meet her daughter. "D," and Cashmere would have to raise her child. All these thoughts were flooding her brain.

It was just too much for one person to deal with. How would Cashmere and "D" handle raising the baby if she wasn't around? Would the baby remember her? Tears kept falling down her face. Life just seemed to be so unfair sometimes. It was not supposed to go down this way, or was it? Never in a million years would she have thought her world would face this situation. She looked around the room at the three people she loved most. Thought this could be the last time she would ever see them. "D" had captured her heart. He was her everything, yet she hadn't had a lifetime to spend with him. Uncle Herbert was her favorite uncle. He was always there for her whenever she needed him. Even now, he was right here with her. Cashmere was her big sister. Sometimes she was hard on her, but deep down, she knew that her big sister loved her dearly. She was about to bring a life into the world and was unsure if she would still be alive to see her.

Chapter 9

Seven o'clock on the dot, her phone rang. "Char, it's Antonio. I am in the lobby. Would you like me to come up, or shall I meet you down here?" "I'll be right down." She grabbed her purse and headed out the door. Entering the elevator, her excitement rose. She liked what she knew about Antonio so far. When she stepped out of the elevator, she immediately saw him. He cleaned up nicely. She really liked what she saw. He met her halfway, reached for her hand, and kissed it. "Hello, Char! It is very nice to see you again!" They both smiled. "Hello to you as well, Antonio. You look very nice." "Thank you, as do you. Shall we?" Antonio reached for her hand again. This time, he held it and guided her towards the front of the hotel. He nodded, and the hotel valet opened the door to their limousine. Char wasn't a stranger to riding in limos, but she didn't expect to be riding with him in one. Obviously, he was trying to impress her. Little did he know that she would have been more impressed if he had shown up in his car. She smiled and walked towards the limo. When she got in, he had sprung for the works. They loaded the limo with all the essentials and much, much more. Antonio nodded to the driver, and the limo pulled off. "Where are we going for dinner?" Char asked. "It's a surprise. It's somewhere that you may not have been before." Char sort of smiled and laughed a little. He knew she was well-traveled, so there weren't many places she hadn't been. She decided not to challenge him and just see where he was taking her. She likes surprises anyway. The limo pulled in between some very tall gates. Drove up this somewhat long and winding driveway. She thought about what type of restaurant would be up here. Her curiosity piqued. She stayed quiet to see where this was leading. When the limo stopped, it was in front of a magnificent mansion. She looked at Antonio, and he asked: "Are you ready?" She smiled and said, "I hope so." Still unsure, she got out of the limo. Antonio took her hand and said, "Trust me, I got you!" She smiled and let him lead her. They walked through the mansion, which was beautiful. On the outside, she could see a helicopter waiting for them. Antonio was pulling out all the stops. She was curious to see just what he had in store. They boarded the helicopter. The pilot took off, and away they flew. By now, Antonio knew Char was more than curious.

He knew she wanted to ask where they were going. He had decided he wouldn't offer any information. They flew for twenty minutes, then the helicopter landed on a yacht. The pilot opened the door to let them out, and Antonio took her hand once again. He led her to a gorgeous candlelit table. Pulled her chair out for her and waited for her to sit down. He walked around to his seat and sat down. A waiter came over and poured wine into both of their glasses. "Okay, Antonio, I have to ask. Just what do you have planned for tonight?" "We said we would have dinner, right?" He replied. "Yes, dinner. This is a little much, though." "I'm sorry. Would you like to do something else?" "No, this is fine. I know you went through a lot of trouble to set this up. It's just a little shocking, that's all." "Why is it shocking? This is the life we are privy to living? Isn't it?" Char didn't really know how to take that comment. Although it was truthful, it seemed like he was bragging or somewhat conceited. She shook it off and decided to just go with things. The night might be great. Time would tell, though. "Possibly," she answered. Antonio wondered if his statement had made her feel a little uncomfortable. The waiter brought out some crab cakes as appetizers. He refilled their wine glasses before leaving the table. Char was more than pleased with the crab cakes. They were delicious. Antonio couldn't help but notice how beautiful she looked tonight.

He wanted to just devour her. He knew he had to play his cards right because she didn't strike him as an easy lay like so many others had been. The waiter placed lobster Thermidor, mushroom risotto, asparagus, and garlic bread in front of her. She smiled, thinking she had eaten this same meal many times. She gave him "A" for effort, though. He was trying to impress her. Was there a motive behind this? Was he up to something? Did he always treat his first dates this way? Char kept going with the evening. So far, the crab cakes and lobster were excellent. The wine was tasty. Glass three had been poured, and the effects kicked in from the first two glasses. "Would you like to take a walk on the deck? Maybe look out on the water." Antonio suggested. "That would be lovely. Let's do it." She replied. They grabbed their glasses of wine and walked toward the deck. It was a beautiful night. The moon was full and glowed. The water was calm, looking almost like a glass. This was romantic. "You look divine, Char. Thank you for having dinner with me tonight. The pleasure is all mine." "You are very welcome, Antonio. This has been a great evening." Antonio put his arms around her waist and said, "The night is still young, so it can only get better. This is a beautiful view, although it is not as beautiful as you!" Before she could reply, he leaned in and kissed her. She kissed him back, then pulled away. Antonio pulled her closer and continued to kiss her.

He let his hand slide down to her backside. It surprised her, letting it stay there for a second. Then she moved his hand away. "We are not there yet," she said. "I thought you liked me, Char." "I like you, Antonio, but that doesn't mean I will sleep with you on our first date. As a matter of fact, I think I should leave. Could you please have the pilot take me back?" "Char, don't leave. Sorry if I offended you. I thought things were going so well. I shouldn't have touched you like that. It won't happen again." She thought about it for a second and said: "If you promise, I'll stay." "I promise, Char. I promise." The waiter came with more wine. He refilled Antonio's, but Char declined. "May I please have water?" she asked. "Of course!" The waiter replied. When he returned with the water, Antonio asked: "Would you like dessert?" Before answering, Antonio motioned for the waiter to bring the dessert. I thought we could have dessert here. He turned on the light, and she saw an all-white grand piano with a bottle of champagne. They situated the piano on a raised platform in the center of the room. Char walked over to the piano to get a closer look. Antonio was right behind her, enjoying the beautiful view. "So, do you play the piano, Char?" Antonio asked. "I play a little." "Well, sit down. Let's see what you're made of." "That sounds a little like a challenge," Char stated. "Not a challenge at all. I want to see how you tickle those keys." Char sat down and pressed her fingers against the ebony and ivory keys. The sound that rose from her playing the piano was melodic and impressive. Antonio sat beside her on the piano bench, looked over at her, and said, "That was wonderful. You are both beautiful and talented." Looking back at Antonio, and couldn't help but think he was still trying to get his way with her. She knew he would break her heart into a million pieces if she gave him a chance. She had sized Antonio up from the beginning of the date. For all she knew, the mansion, the helicopter, and the yacht didn't belong to him. Antonio only wanted one thing from her, and his game wasn't strong enough for her not to know it. "Antonio?" "Yes, Char." "This has been a wonderful evening, but it is getting late, and I have an early flight in the morning." "Char, the night is still young, though. We haven't even started the music yet. I would like a chance to hold you in my arms and slow dance with you." Char cracked a smile with a slight laugh that followed. "What's so funny?" "Okay, Antonio, here is what is so funny. You have gotten me twisted. Apparently, you think I am the type of woman that will sleep with a man on the first date. You have gone through all this trouble to impress me, and all you really had to do was let me get to know you. I had a nice evening, but I am ready to return to my hotel now. Please have your pilot take me back." "Char, come on now. You know it's not like that at all.

It's true, I wanted to impress you. It wasn't because of what you think, though." "Okay, Antonio. You're right. I would still like to leave, though." "Fine, Char! You would have been lousy in bed anyway!" "One thing is for certain, Antonio; you will never know. Will you?" Char got up, walked out of the room, and headed for the helicopter. The pilot was standing by the helicopter when she walked up. "Could you please take me back to the airport?" "Of course, ma'am. I would be happy to do so." The pilot answered. He opened the door for Char. As she was getting in, Antonio was walking up. "Char, please forgive me. I didn't mean it." He shouted as the pilot was closing the door. The pilot walked around to the other side, got in the helicopter, and away they flew. "Why do you want to go to the airport?" The pilot asked. "I need to arrange transportation back to the hotel." "Ma'am, I can take you back to the mansion, then drive you back to the hotel." "Well, I wouldn't want to impose on Antonio any more than I have already." "What do you mean by that?" "I feel bad using his services while not being with him." The pilot laughed hysterically. "His services, his services. That's a good one." He said in between laughter. "What is so funny?" Char asked. "Antonio doesn't have any services. Antonio is the grandson of a filthy rich real estate tycoon. Everything you saw tonight, including this helicopter, is the property of Graham Jordan." Char laughed too. She had been right all along. Antonio was a poser. "Okay, if you don't mind taking me to the mansion, then driving me to my hotel, I would be fine with that," Char said. "No problem, ma'am. I would be happy to do just that. Might I say, I love the way you handled him, too? Most women fall for his game and sleep with him in the piano room. You are definitely a cut above the rest!" "Thank you very much. I really appreciate that." "If you are thirsty, we are only ten minutes away from the mansion. We'll radio ahead and have whatever you want put in the limo." "I am fine. Appreciate the gesture, though. I have had enough to eat and drink already. I want to get back to the hotel and rest." "Okay, I will make sure you get back safely." Char smiled and gazed out the window at the beautiful mansion before they landed.

Chapter 10

The following day, Char boarded the plane and headed back to Virginia. She was ready to get home and just relax for two days. A break was needed for quality time with her girls. She eased her seat back when the plane took off and closed her eyes for some much-needed rest. When she arrived in Virginia, it was six in the evening. It felt good to touch that Virginia soil, home sweet home. She got in the limo waiting for her, kicked off her shoes, and grabbed water. The driver drove off, and she looked out the window at the beautiful Virginia scenery as the limo made its way to her place. Although she had been all over the world, there was no better place for her to be than home. Virginia was comforting to her. Knowing that was the one place she could let her hair down and just be plain ole Char. Not being glammed up unless that was wanted. She could just chill and kick it with her girls. That's why she remained in Virginia. She could have been like many celebrities and moved away to New York or California. Still, she wanted to be where she was comfortable. And she was most comfortable in the VA. The driver opened her door and got her bags when she got home. After bringing them to the door, she told him, "That's fine. I can get them from here. Thanks and have a great evening." She handed him a hundred-dollar bill. He smiled and said, "Thank you very much!" He turned around, walked towards the car, and Char entered the house and dropped her bags at the door. She let out the most enormous sigh. It relieved her to be home.

Chapter 11

Ingrid lay in the bed, tears rolling down her face. Her contractions were becoming more and more unbearable. Cashmere and Uncle Herbert were each holding Ingrid's hands. Cashmere could not hold back her tears. Uncle Herbert was still in disbelief that Ingrid's life was in jeopardy. Damion was sitting in the chair, hoping everything would work out for Ingrid. Even though he wasn't ready to be a father, he would do his best to keep his promise to Ingrid. Cashmere still had an unpleasant taste in her mouth about Damion. She knew he wasn't about anything in school. She figured he still wasn't about anything as an adult. Though Ingrid thought the world of him. To Ingrid, he was the air she breathed! No one could tell her any differently, either. Even though she didn't want to, Cashmere had to admit to herself that he still looked very nice. She could see why Ingrid was so attracted to him. Ingrid screamed in agony as the next contraction set in. The nurse ran into the room. "Is everything okay here?" The nurse asked. "Her contractions are hurting her. Isn't there anything you can do for her?" Uncle Herbert said. "I'll get the doctor to see if he can recheck her." Ingrid tried to be strong, but those contractions were hard to withstand. Her face told the story of just how much pain she was in. Cashmere found it hard to see her little sister struggle like this. Ingrid had been through so much for so long. It amazed Cashmere at how she was still hanging in there. She would do anything to trade places with her so that Ingrid wouldn't have to suffer so much. The doctor came into the room to check Ingrid. After looking, the doctor noted that the baby hadn't turned. It was still breached, and the cord was tightening around the neck. "We have to deliver this baby now. Please have operating room five set up stat." The doctor yelled! "Ingrid, the baby needs to be delivered now. We can't wait any longer. We have to take you to the operating room now." "Okay, doc. Please make sure my baby makes it. I don't care about me, but make sure my baby is okay." Ingrid said. "Ingrid, everything will be fine. Don't worry, we'll take care of everything!" the doctor said. The nurse came in with the OR Tech. "We need to take her over now!" The nurse said. They rolled the bed out of the room. "Wait, just wait one minute! Ingrid, I love you. You can do this! I'll be here when you get back!" Damion said. Ingrid looked over and smiled at everyone. "I love you guys. See you soon!" Then they rolled Ingrid to operating room five. Uncle Herbert and Cashmere hugged one another. Uncle Herbert looked over at Damion and said: "Come on, Ingrid wouldn't want it any other way." Damion looked at Uncle Herbert, then looked at Cashmere. Cashmere nodded for him to come over. He walked over and joined them in a hug. "Thank you for allowing me to come into your family. I know things weren't the best for us in high school, Cashmere, but I am glad you are opening up to Ingrid and me." "Damion, please believe I haven't allowed you into our family. There is no choice for me. I have to do what Ingrid asked me to do. I am trying to be there for her." "However you want to look at it, Cashmere, I appreciate it, just the same," Damion said. Cashmere just looked at him. She wasn't sure what to make of him. She wasn't ready to be forgiving him right now. She still wanted him to know just how much she still despised him. Her thoughts returned her to a pleasant time with her girls. Those were the good times. That's when she didn't have to worry about all the drama that was going on now. Back when Ingrid was just an annoying little sister. Now, she has bigger problems. Way bigger problems to consider. Adding Damion to the picture was mind-blowing. Ingrid had been in the OR for ten minutes, and

Damion was already getting on Cashmere's nerves. How would she ever fulfill her promise to her sister if Ingrid didn't survive all this? If only this was some freakish nightmare... this couldn't be farther from reality. Just then, Damion's phone rang. He looked at the phone and excused himself from the room. Uncle Herbert and Cashmere looked at each other. They were both thinking the same thing. "Who in the hell is he talking to?" Cashmere stepped out of the room to check for herself. She saw Damion walking up the hallway. She saw him enter the cafeteria, where he sat beside a woman. "Oh hell no, this isn't going down like this!" Cashmere shouted as she walked upon them. "Damion, who the hell is this woman you're sitting with while my sister is up there fighting for her life to give birth to your child?" Both Damion and the young lady looked up at Cashmere. "Cashmere, what's going on with you?" "I asked you a question. Don't play it off! Who is this woman?" "Excuse me, do you have a problem?" The young lady questioned, "Do I have a problem? You better ask your lame-ass man that question?" "My man?" Both Damion and the young lady laughed. "Since you must know, Damion is not my man; he is my cousin. He told me about Ingrid having the baby. You would have noticed that I was wearing a hospital uniform if you weren't so busy running your mouth." "Cousin? You work here?" "Yes, cousin. Yes, I work here. Cashmere, have a seat and join us. You must be going through it." "I apologize for my rudeness. Right now, I am going through a lot. I will admit, I don't trust Damion. I haven't really cared for him since high school. So I immediately thought the worse when I saw him leave after his phone rang. I thought he was cheating on my sister." Damion looked at Cashmere and said, "You have got to let the past go. You can't move forward holding onto it." "I'm Deborah; sorry for my rude behavior. You caught me off guard, and I overreacted." "No, it's all good. I had it coming. I was out of pocket." "You think." Damion added. Cashmere shot Damion a look that screamed: "Don't mess with me!" Damion was going to take any mess off of Cashmere any longer. He shot a look right back at her. He had put up with her stuff for long enough. There was more to this than just what Cashmere thought or felt. It was time for Damion to give her a piece of his mind. "Cashmere, check this out. I am so sorry for how things turned out between us in high school. Understand, we were both kids and knew nothing about life. I was just having a good time, the best way I could. I thought you were about the same thing. Do you know how the life of a jock can be? I was about that life back then. It didn't take me long to realize that things shouldn't have been the way they were. I need to thank you. I would have continued to live that way if it weren't for you. I wouldn't have gotten my act together." "So, you thank me by getting with my sister?" "Actually, I didn't know she was your sister until I walked in the door." "And how is that? She didn't talk about her family to you?" "Yes, she did. She referred to you as "C." Sorry, I didn't put it all together until I walked into the room tonight." "Wow, she referred to you as "D." I wonder if that was on purpose. If she did it because she knew we had a past." "She realized it after it was too late," Deborah said. "Anyway, can we make amends now, Cashmere? I don't want to go on like this. We are family now and must act like family, especially for Ingrid and the baby." Cashmere looked at Damion, then at Deborah. Deborah smiled and looked at Cashmere. "Damion, this is very hard for me. I have to be honest. I am having a hard time with this. I can't really give you an answer right now. Before I answer you, I need to think about it a bit. With that, Cashmere excused herself and walked away. "Cashmere?" Damion yelled out. Cashmere turned around. "Take your time; I understand!" Damion said. Cashmere smiled slightly, turned, and walked away. "Wow, she is a trip. Nobody to play with, that's for certain." Damion said. "You got that right, baby. We have to be careful with her. Did you like how I came up with the cousin thing off the cuff?" "Yeah, that was good. Where did you get Deborah from, though?" Babe, I have a cousin named Deborah." "How funny?" "So, when can

I see you again, baby?" "Let me see how things play out here, and I will call you later." "That's cool. I get off at midnight. If you want to swing through, I'll leave the key in the normal place." "That's cool, Bree. I should get back now." Damion got up and walked away. Bree watched him the whole time he was leaving. He knew he was playing with fire. If Cashmere ever found out, he would get burned. He had feelings for Ingrid. Although, she wasn't what he wanted in a woman. She got pregnant right before he broke up with her, and he didn't have the heart to go through with it once he found out. Now he was having a baby with a woman he didn't want to be with and probably couldn't be with after tonight. Yes, it was a morbid thought, but until he walked in the room tonight, it was his out. Now he has to deal with Cashmere's 5150 ass for eternity. Before he walked back into the room, he got his thoughts together, knowing he had to play the game from here on out. He took a deep breath and pushed the door open to see Cashmere and Uncle Herbert in prayer. He tried to be as quiet as possible to let them finish. Uncle Herbert opened his eyes, seeing Damion by the door. He extended his hand for him to join them. Damion walked over to them and joined in prayer. When it was over, they all said, "Amen." Cashmere was crying. Uncle Herbert didn't want to let their hands go. It was as if he was giving and receiving the strength they needed to overcome all this. Damion looked at both of them. His guilt was increasing. He felt a heavy burden on his shoulders. Maybe if he explained, they would understand. He knew that this wasn't the time to say anything, though. The question was whether there would be a right time to discuss this. This would be detrimental to the situation. Cashmere would never forgive him. Uncle Herbert would surely hate him. How would he be able to see his child? Here's another thought... What if Ingrid survived all this?

Chapter 12

Rico missed Tammy more than he had ever thought he would. Her trip was almost over, but it seemed like he still had forever to wait. He wanted her back now; Rico needed her back now. He tried his best not to disturb her while she was on vacation, but he felt like a little child missing his favorite toy. Even though he loved her, he knew how much he cared about her. He hadn't been in a situation where he had to miss her until now. He missed her sexy voice, her touch, her sweet kisses. Just having her around was what he missed. She was his everything, and it didn't take her being away from him to know it, either. He desperately wanted to pick up the phone to talk to her. Just to hear her voice. He would try his best to maintain and not bother her. Let her enjoy what she had left of her trip. When she returned, though, she was his for a few days. Rico needed that, and he hoped she needed it. He tried to concentrate on other things to take his mind off how much he missed her. He had planned to go by the club today to do a little paperwork that kept him busy and focused on accomplishing his goal of owning a restaurant. Plus, he knew R.J. could use the help. Since he'd met Tammy, his presence at the club was minimal. Luckily, R.J. didn't care about his absence or hadn't mentioned it. R.J. was good about things like that. Whenever the pieces were down, R.J. was the first to step in and pick them up. The club had been doing a lot of business in the last few months. The place was busy every night. Friday and Saturday were their heaviest nights. So much so that they had to increase their orders on Mondays, getting them through the weekends. Business was good; it was great! When he got there, R.J. was not there. He went into the office and went over the paperwork from the weekend. The numbers were great. They profited six thousand from Thursday to Sunday. Fifteen hundred was from the door, and the rest was the bar and food. R.J. was definitely handling business. It impressed Rico with the way things were going. He wished he had played more of a part. Business had never been this good while he was managing. Was R.J. a better manager than him? Had he been holding the club back all this time? Many thoughts were moving through his head. Then the door opened, and R.J. walked in. "What's up, man? How have you been?" R.J. said as he dapped Rico up. "I have been good, thanks. And you, my brother?" "Been busy, lots going on around here. I have to catch you up on things. Business is off the chain right now." "Yeah, I see. I have been looking at the books from the weekend. Man, things are going really well." "Yeah, we implemented changes that have really taken off." "Like what? What changes?" "Well, we sell steak, rib, and chicken dinners from six to eight. That gets people in the door early, staying for the club. Lines back up around seven forty-five. When the club starts at nine, people normally wait to get in. We keep a constant line out front until closing." "How do you keep the lines outside for so long?" "Oh, that was an easy one. Every eighth customer in line gets in free." "Not too bad, not too bad at all. How did you come up with that idea?" "I thought about all the lines I have waited in and figured it would be nice if someone could get in free after all that waiting. I chose the number eight because it seemed like a good enough number. Anyway, it has been working so far." "All that sounds great. I'm glad you implemented those changes. I wish I could have helped you with them, though." "It's all good. Actually, I wish you could have helped me with them too. I kinda miss having my boy around to handle things with me. That brings me to a question, though." "What is it, dawg?" "I know you've been spending time with Tammy. You must be serious about her. Okay, here goes... are you still interested in running the business? If not, I can buy you out and do this myself." "Hell yeah, I am still interested. Why wouldn't I be?" "Well, you're never here anymore. I figured you'd changed your mind and would rather be with her than be a part of the business." "My bad, dawg. Should have been more involved. I am sorry. I guess I got my priorities mixed up. Don't worry, my brother; the club will have my full attention going forward." "It doesn't need your full attention. The two of us can run it. It needs more attention than you've been giving it. I know you are serious about Tammy. I don't want to interfere with that, but I want you to know that it takes both of us to run this club. You feel me?" "Yeah, I feel you." "Good, we cool?" "Yeah, we're cool." With that, R.J. went to the stockroom to prep the bar for the night. He needed to pull Jack, Hennessey, Vodka, and a few other bottles from the stockroom. After R.J. left the office, Rico wondered about the conversation that had just taken place. Was R.J. trying to get the club for himself, or was he trying to get Rico back into the club? Rico knew he had to return to being focused on whatever R.J.'s reasonings were. How would that affect his time with Tammy, though? Hopefully, she would be as understanding as he hoped she would be. One never knew how someone would react to unwanted change. One thing is certain: he could devote his time to the club while she was still on the trip.

He would deal with this conversation when she returned. Rico kept looking over the paperwork. He continued to be impressed by how well the club was doing without his constant involvement. The office phone rang. "The Crib," this is Rico; how may I help you?" "Yeah, I need to speak to R.J.!" "Who's calling, please?" "Just get R.J.; you need not know who I am to do that." Rico looked at the phone, wondering what this was all about. "Hold on, please." Rico put the caller on hold and got up to get R.J. When he saw him, he told him someone was on the phone for him. "Who is it?" R.J. asked. "Man, I don't know. They didn't want to give me their name. Whoever they are, they are tripping." R.J. went to the office and closed the door behind him. Rico was behind him but stopped when R.J. closed the door. Whoever was on the phone, R.J. needed to speak to in private. Rico heard R.J. locking the door. He walked over to the bar and poured himself some orange juice. A few minutes later, R.J. came out of the office. "Yo man, what was up with that phone call?" "Awe, nothing, man, I handled it." "Handled what?" "It was just a vendor calling about a missed payment." "Didn't seem like a vendor, R.J." "Rico, if I said it was a vendor, it was a vendor. Stop tripping!" R.J. walked away, leaving Rico wondering if he was telling the truth or not. They had a big night ahead of them. It was Friday, and the crowd would come in about three hours. D.J. Funk Funk was premiering tonight. He was one of the hottest d.j. s in the Richmond area. His following and their normal weekend crowd would make for a fantastic night. R. J. had increased the staff by almost double to ensure the guests were cared for. Some staff came to help set up and prepare for the big night. R.J. came back to the bar to restock. He expected a busy night, so he wanted to ensure there was more than enough on hand. The hope was that the bar would be close to empty by the night's end. That would make for a great night. The kitchen was preparing to serve at least one hundred dinners. That might be a tall order, but they were hopeful. R.J. thought it was good that Rico was here. That way, he could see exactly how business had picked up since the last time he had been around. When R.J. finished restocking the bar, D.J. FunkFunk arrived to set up his equipment. "Where do you want me to set up?" "What's up, FunkFunk? You can set up over there," Rico said. "Rico, it's been a minute since I've seen you. How are things? Where were you, dawg?" R.J. looked at FunkFunk and Rico. "Funk, man, I've been around. Just doing some different things. How have you been?" "Man, I've been good. It's good to see you, my brother. Let me get over here and set this equipment up. I'll talk to you before I get out of here tonight." "Okay, sounds cool. Good luck tonight!" "Thanks! I have something special planned for tonight.

Trust me, it will be on." "Handle your business!" With that, Funk Funk set up his equipment. "Man, it has been a minute since I've seen Funk. How did you get him to do his thing here?" Rico asked R.J., "Let's just say we have some same people in common." "Oh, okay. That's good to know." "Why is that?" R.J. asked. "Because Funk and I go way back, we also have some same people in common." "Sounds like we are just one big happy family," R.J. said sarcastically. Rico laughed while walking away to let R.J. finish whatever he was doing. Rico couldn't help but think something seemed different about him. He seemed distant, as if he was hiding something. He also knew that Funk ran with some unsavory people. That was a life that Rico had left a long time ago. A life he wasn't very proud of. That's why it had been time since he had seen Funk. If R.J. was dealing with Funk, then something had definitely changed. Rico needed to find out what was happening before something crazy went down. He knew he couldn't ask R.J., but Funk might give him the needed information. He figured he would talk to him after the night was over. The truth worried him about what R.J. might have gotten into, not to mention the business. He wondered how much R.J. knew about Funk and the people he rolled with. His guess was not much at all. He figured that if R.J. knew about Funk, he wouldn't be dealing with him. At least, he hoped that was the case.

That was the only reason he figured R.J. was doing business with him. Since R.J. was dealing with Funk, there would definitely be problems down the road they would have to deal with. When Rico returned to the office to check on some paperwork he was working on, he saw R.J. on the phone. By the way, things sounded. It seemed as if whoever he was talking to was quite upset. He slammed the phone down and screamed "shit" before walking out of the office. Rico checked the phone to see who he was talking to. He recognized the number as one of Funk's associates named Slick. Slick was truly a bad dude. I otherwise knew him as the collector. If Slick had been involved, things must be worse than he initially thought. Slick only came into play when money was delinquent. Which meant that R.J. owed them money, and they would come to collect soon. Rico opened the office door and saw Funk and R.J. talking. He knew they were talking about the phone call, which meant they were discussing the money. Rico walked over, and they both got quiet. R.J. walked backed to the office and shut the door. "What was that all about, Funk?" Rico asked. "Maybe you should ask your boy." "Come on, Funk, I am asking you. What's going on, man?" "All right, look, homie. Your boy is into us for twenty-five large. We want our money. So, I am here to get our money. He has until the weekend to get us the money, or Slick will visit him to collect it. And you already know how Slick gets down!" "You know we will not make twenty-five large in a weekend." "To be honest, Rico, that's not our problem. It's his. He knew the business deal when he accepted the terms." "Come on, Funk, you have got to give us more time. At least another couple of weeks." "You know I can't do that, Rico. Besides, it's not up to me anymore. Once Slick gets involved, there's no turning back." "Funk, it's me, man. It's Rico! You know we go back. That's my boy. He doesn't have a clue what he's done. Do me a solid on this one." "Rico, you know we go back, and I would do what I can for you. I can't do that, man. He's going to be stubborn on this one." "Funk, let me go and holla at him. I'll be back in a minute. Go nowhere!" "I'll give you ten minutes." Rico went to the office. "R.J., what's going on, man? Did you borrow money from Funk?" "Well, if you already know, why are you asking?" "What happened? Why did you need to borrow money from them?" "The business was sinking. We were losing money on the weekends, so I needed to invest funds I didn't have." "Man, I wish you had chatted with me before you did that. We could have explored some other options." "Well, you weren't here, so I had to decide myself." "You know you could have called me." "You should have been here. You were running behind some skirt." "Watch yourself. She's not just a skirt. That's my lady." "Whatever, she's the reason you're not around. She's the reason we did not include you in the decision." "Man, these cats aren't playing. They will come for you and anybody you love." "I'll get them their money. Don't you worry about it?" "How? How will you get them their money by Sunday?" "Sunday?" "Yeah, Sunday is when Slick comes to collect the twenty-five large." "I thought I had until next weekend." "No, my brother, you have until this Sunday."

Chapter 13

After, the Captain's feast was over. The three girls went to get a much-needed massage. While they were being relaxed by their masseuses, Char filled them in on her horrible date with Antonio. She told them he was excellent in the beginning. He said all the right things right until they went out. She admitted she was feeling him, then he took a turn for the worse when he mistook her for a one-night stand. He tried too hard to impress her with his grandfather's money. The funny part was that she had enough money to buy and sell him several times. Did he not know how wealthy she was, or did he? It didn't really matter if he did or not since she didn't fall for his madness. She told her girls that the best part of the night was when the date was over. "He totally sounds a little full of himself," Tammy said. They all laughed at the thought of Antonio getting with Char on the first night. Obviously, he didn't know who he was dealing with. Char was definitely not that woman. She was about getting to know someone before taking things to that level. That's why she didn't have many relationships. The men didn't want to take the time to get to know her; they wanted to lay and play with her. Men like that weren't worth her time nor her love. She was determined to give her mind, body, and soul to someone who not only deserved her but would love her madly. She was a queen looking for her king to ascend their throne together.

"So, what's been going on with you ladies?" Char asked. "We have been trying to enjoy this vacation. It's been hard to do because we worry about Ingrid and the baby. The best thing is that you joined us for the rest of the cruise." Stephanie said. "How is Ingrid doing? Have you heard from Cashmere?" "I haven't heard from her since she got back to Virginia. I figure that no news is good news. I will contact Cashmere when we get back." Tammy said. There was a certain silence that befell the room. All the girls knew this phone call couldn't wait another few days. Everybody needed to know exactly what was going on with Ingrid. If it was severe enough for Cashmere to leave the ship, then it must be important enough for them to call and check on her. The only problem was that neither of them wanted to be the one to make that call. No one wanted to hear exactly how serious her condition was.

This was far too much for either of them to think about dealing with right now. The time to deal with it would come soon enough. They would all have to be vital for Ingrid. Tammy's phone buzzed. She looked down and saw Cashmere had sent a text. The time had come for them to find out about Ingrid's situation.

Cashmere... Hey Tammy, how are you?

Tammy... I am good. How are you and Ingrid doing?

Cashmere... Well, I am a bundle of nerves. Ingrid is having a rough time right now.

Tammy... What is going on?

Cashmere... Well, she is having complications with the delivery. So the baby is a breach. It's also premature, and they discovered Ingrid has heart issues.

Tammy... Oh my goodness. What is the doctor saying?

Cashmere... Well, the doctors are being cautious. They think this will be a very trying delivery for her.

Tammy... A very trying delivery for her. What does that mean?

Cashmere... That means her complications are severe, and she might not make it. My sister could die from having this baby.

Tammy... GOD, no! This can't be happening!

Char and Stephanie were reading the texts with Tammy. Neither of them could believe their eyes.

Cashmere... I wish it wasn't Tammy. This is unbelievable. I don't really know what to do.

Tammy... All you can do is be there for her. Comfort her as much as you can.

Cashmere... I am. I wish I could do more than that. I hope I can make it all better for her!

Tammy... We can only do what we can do. We will keep her in our prayers!

Cashmere... We appreciate that. Tell the girls we said hi.

Tammy... They said hi. Take care of Ingrid and yourself. We will see both of you soon!

Cashmere... Okay, see ya soon!

Char's eyes filled with tears at the thought of Ingrid's situation. They had known Ingrid since she was a little girl. They had watched her grow into the young lady she is now. No one deserved to have this happen to them. Especially Ingrid. Her life was just beginning. The girls tried to get themselves together. Tried to get their composure back. This was too much for them to deal with. Hopefully, Ingrid would make it through this with no more problems. Things needed to get back to normal. Their lives have been through so much over the past few months.

Chapter 14

"Ingrid, please count from ten to one." The anesthesiologists said. By the time Ingrid got to two, the anesthesia had taken effect, and Ingrid was out. The doctor made the incision across her abdomen; he carefully positioned one hand around the baby's head and the other on the umbilical cord. The doctor gently removed the cord from the baby's neck. Once free from the cord, he maneuvered the baby to face downwards. He looked over at Ingrid's vitals, which were much lower than they should have been. Ingrid's complications had worsened. He returned his attention to the baby. After pulling the baby out, he clamped off the umbilical cord and cut it.

The delivery room technician took the baby over to the incubator and took care of the baby. Before he could finish, the baby took a turn for the worst. The technician alerted the nurse. The nurse grabbed the baby and took her to the NICU to save her. Meanwhile, the doctor was busy trying to close up Ingrid. Her heart rate was steadily dropping; it had fallen drastically low. The doctor asked the nurse to get the crash cart. They had to do something now to save this girl. Her life was in the doctor's hands now. She was on the brink of death. Could he bring her back from there? It would take a miracle to do so. Hopefully, Ingrid had enough strength to fight for her life. Cause she would have to do so.

Cashmere, Uncle Herbert, and Damion were in the hospital room, waiting on Ingrid's return. They had no clue she had taken a turn for the worse. All they could do was hope and pray that both Ingrid and the baby would be all right. They all knew this was a long shot for both of them, with the premature baby and Ingrid's heart condition. They both had an uphill climb to survive. This was their darkest moment. This was the hour of despair for their family. Damion could only sit and wonder how much of this he could take. He contemplated if he was ready to take all of this on. He knew that if he did, there would be no turning back. Cashmere would be forever in his life to torment him and make him feel like a miserable piece of shit. Cashmere thought to herself that this would be a long hard road for them if Ingrid didn't make it.

She wasn't ready for all of this. She wasn't prepared to be an aunt, much less a mother. How did they all end up here? Things spiraled out of normalcy rather quickly for them. First, Ingrid meets a guy, then she's pregnant. Complications arise with the pregnancy, then we find out she has a heart condition. On top of all that, the father is an ex-boyfriend of Cashmere from high school. Now, she may face raising a child with him.

How could all this be happening right now? Uncle Herbert had a lot on his mind. He had to speak with Cashmere about some missing finances to see if she knew what had happened. Now wasn't the time for it, though. He needed to be there for Ingrid. She needed all the support she could get right now. Life had dealt her a raw deal, and it would take everything short of a miracle to see her through it. He wondered about this Damion character. What role did he play in all of this? Did he know that Ingrid and Cashmere were sisters the whole time? Would he really be there for Ingrid when she needed him? There was something about Damion that Uncle Herbert just didn't like. It wasn't because he had dated Cashmere in high school. He knew things like that happened. There was something about Damion's eyes that just didn't seem right to Uncle Herbert. Damion had a story to tell, and Uncle Herbert knew it.

In the NICU. Ingrid's little girl was going through her own issues. Her breathing was shallow. Her coloration was off; she was in trouble. The nurses were doing everything they could to help the baby. She had a long road to recovery, and it was just beginning. She had been in this world for thirty minutes and was already struggling to stay in it. Her color had increased. She was looking better, but the fight was still ongoing. She needed medication intravenously to keep her from getting worse. The nurses needed to feed her often to keep her strength up so she would gain weight. This baby was in the fight for her life. The poor child didn't even know what was in store for her. They also needed to rule out any disabilities that might have occurred because of the premature birth and the cord wrapped around her neck. They had to do a full workup on the baby to ensure all her vital organs were functioning. Finally, there was positivity; the baby's color looked much better. That meant she was getting the proper amount of oxygen. Her chances of living were increasing. Prospects were looking up for this little girl. Hanging on to her life. She was fighting, fighting for her life!

Chapter 15

Rico explained to R.J. just how bad the situation was for them. "Man, I used to run with Funk and them. I know how they do things. You have no idea just how serious this is for us. Slick is going to come here, looking for you. He will demand the twenty-five large if you don't have it. At the very least, he is going to break some bones." "Rico, I thought this was a good thing for the club. I was really trying to get ahead and make things work. When the club started losing money, I had to do something. Funk had come to the club on a Saturday and introduced himself to me as a deejay. He said he wanted to play in the club and had a business proposition for me. I didn't realize that it was going to turn out like this. I didn't realize that he was a shady individual. Man, all I wanted was to make this club a success. Just trying to build the brand, my brother, trying to build the brand." "I understand all of that, R.J. I wish you would have spoken to me about it before you made this move. Now we have to deal with this, and unless you have the twenty-five large, we will have to devise a plan to get us out of this."

"Rico, I am sure it will all work out." "I don't think you understand the magnitude of this situation, my brother. This isn't some bill collector that you can make payment arrangements with. This is the MOB. This is one of Richmond's most notorious gangs that you are in cahoots with." "I will admit, I did not realize who I was dealing with. I didn't have a reason to doubt his intentions until I had already accepted the money. That's when everything got real. The business is doing well. Most of the money has been earned back. We just need another ten grand. I'm not sure if that will happen by Sunday, though." "Okay, do you have any funds that you can contribute to this fiasco?" "I have a couple of grand that I can put towards it, but I would need to get that money back from the company at some point." "Come on, R.J., a couple of grand. We both know you have more than that. You got us into this mess, so you must do your best to get us out of it." "Yeah, I hear you. You have to understand that I did all this to better the club. Our club!" "Was it our club when you contacted these goons without my knowledge?" "Okay, I think we are getting off track here. This conversation is supposed to be about paying this money by Sunday, not about placing blame." "You're exactly right. We need to stay focused on the situation at hand. So, how will we get the rest of the money by Sunday? Do you have a plan?" "Honestly, no, I don't have a plan. We'll come up with something, though." "Whatever we come up with, better be really good. We need to come up with it really fast too!" "I know that's right. We only have a couple of days left to do it." "Okay, I need to go out here and see if I can talk Funk into giving us some more time."

Rico left the office and went out to talk to Funk again. "Yo Funk, what's up? Can we chop it up a little?" "Rico, I think we said all that needs to be said until Sunday." "Come on now, Funk. You know we go way back. This guy is not one of those regular hood dudes you are used to dealing with. We boys. You know I was there when your son was born." "You had to go there, didn't you? Because we go way back, I will talk to Slick to see if I can buy you a couple more days." "Man, that's all we need. I appreciate it." "Now, you know I can't really promise anything. Slick does his own thing, but I do have some influence." "Again, I appreciate anything that you can do for us." Rico, you have to know that this can't happen again. There won't be any more favors like this." "Funk... please believe, we won't have to discuss this again. We will be straight from here on out." "Alright, man, I will talk to him and tell you what he says." "Cool, you know where to find me." "Without a doubt. I'm out!" Funk turned away and headed for the exit. Rico said a quick little prayer that Slick would go for it. They would have to deal with him on a much more dangerous level if he didn't go for it. A level that Rico had left behind some years ago. A level that he didn't want to return to any time soon. He had left that part of his life behind for a reason. He had turned his back on the streets to do things legitimately for once. He returned to the office to let R.J. know the deal. When he entered, R.J. was pacing the floor. He was still worried about making enough money to give to these hoodlums. "So what did he say? Did you handle it? Are we good?" "He said he couldn't promise anything but would talk to Slick about giving us a couple more days to pay." "Man, if he can pull that off, we would be good to go. I know we could have the money by then." "Exactly; he will let me know what Slick says." "When? When is he going to let you know?" "I would imagine as soon as he finds out. I'm sure it will be before Sunday." "I hope so. I hope these fools don't come back on Sunday to press us for the money." "Funk and I go way back. He would give us a heads up if something was going to go down." "Are you sure about that? You just said you turned your back on the streets to go legit. How do you know that he isn't carrying some grudge against you? How do you know he will even talk to Slick on our behalf?" "How do I know? I know because we are boys, and I trust him." "You can't trust a gangster Rico." "Who are you telling that to, man? You trusted him enough to take money from him, and you don't even know him as I do. We have a better chance of getting out of this alive because I talked to him. Had I not, you would be running for your life on Sunday." "Oh, I don't doubt that you made the situation better. I thank you for that. I just don't think that we are in the clear yet. That's all I'm saying. Hell, he could catch Slick on a bad day, then where would we be?" "We would be in the same situation that we were in before I talked to him. I'll tell you what... let's worry about that when or if we get there." "Rico, I hope you are right about this. If you aren't, I could be a dead man." The sad part about that is that you're absolutely right. You will likely have to defend your life if it doesn't work. Slick will come for you, and he won't stop until he gets you! He'll gun down anybody in his path. I have seen the brother put in work. He is relentlessly ruthless, to say the least. I have only seen him stand down once. And that took some doing. You're in luck, though; Funk talked him into that one too." "I hope he can talk him into it again. We just need a few more days, and we should be in the clear." Look, R.J., I need you to promise me something." "What's that?" "If we get through this, please don't ever deal with Funk again." "I promise, no doubt. That goes without saying. You don't even have to worry about that." "I'm sure Funk will come through, but if he doesn't, I have an ace in the hole too!" "An ace in the hole? What do you mean?" "I'd rather not say, just yet. Let's see how things go first. If I need to use it, then I'll tell you at that time." "Alright, as long as there is a plan B." "Oh, there is definitely a plan B. I don't want to go there but will if I have to." "Why don't you want to go there?" "Because if I do, there is no turning back." "What do you mean?" "I mean, bodies will start dropping!" "Oh shit, like that?" "Yeah, like that."

Chapter 16

The Diamond Line had reached Bermuda. They would dock the ship for a full day. It was time for the girls to go see what Bermuda offered. They quickly left the boat and walked toward some stores. There were all types of souvenir shops to look for little trinkets to take home. It was just the thing they needed to take their mind off of Ingrid. They could spend hours shopping and grab something to eat when they were finished. Besides, Stephanie had to get her share of the Bermudian cuisine. There was no way she would come here and not experience this country's delicious food. That was the basis for her taking this vacation. She wanted to try out some extraordinary dishes throughout the cruise. Maybe she would find something that could be added to Rains' menu.

Char found fabrics she thought would surely make a lovely ensemble. She had a knack for creating beautiful fashion. In the past, she had created quite a few garments she was proud of. She had even worn two to some fashion shows. To her surprise, she received several compliments on them. That let her know she might have something to fall back on after her modeling career. She would continue designing and creating clothing so she could one day promote her own fashion line. It would be wonderful to see models wearing her dress as they cascaded down the runway. Just another step in the right direction towards building her brand. She had been in the modeling game for some time now. Her career would wind down in the upcoming years, so she needed another avenue to transition into before her runway days were over. It would be the perfect segue into continuing her life in the fashion industry. So many models before her had done the same thing. She figured, why not continue in their footsteps? They had already opened the door. All she had to do was walk through it, like so many before. She already knew how she wanted her line to be. She wanted something elegant but affordable. Something the hard-working people of the world could afford to wear. There wouldn't be any catering to the rich. This was strictly for the everyday citizen. The people who worked forty hours a week, the people who had to take their kids to soccer practice. The people that didn't have the most significant income but had the greatest desire to wear lovely garments. That is who her line would be for. Remembering when she was a little girl, her parents didn't have much money. They did, however, have a love for clothing. Somehow they always made sure they all had a lovely dress to wear. It wasn't the most expensive, but it looked nice, just the same. Her mother had a way of putting items together and making them look outstanding. That is where she got her love for fashion from her mother. Her mother would spend hours shopping for fabric or shopping for clothing. Char loved it when her mother came home with the material. She would get to help her sew. Her mother made many garments. Everything from shirts to suits.

Char didn't realize it, but she was being groomed for a life in fashion. Looking back, she had come a long way. She is thankful to her parents for always being by her side. To show her what she needed to know to make it in this world. It's a brutal world, even more so for a woman. You must be strong to make it in this world as a woman. As a black woman, getting ahead in this world is vital! Char had proven that she could persevere in this world. She had proven that she could get ahead on her own merit. Now, this adds to her legacy. She would ensure a strong future for the rest of her family. Someday, she would have kids, and her kids would have kids. She wanted to ensure she amassed a hefty enough fortune to last so that her family wouldn't have to struggle like many families do today.

Tammy was enjoying the scenery. There were lots of greenery and beautiful landscapes to catch the eye. The ocean was magnificently mesmerizing. She felt very fortunate to view something so beautiful, something so majestic. Bermuda had tropical views, beautiful people, and most of all. Its beauty had captured her heart. This place was beyond beautiful. It was breathtaking! All she could think was that it would be nice if Cashmere could experience this. This is what all the girls were probably thinking. Tammy could see her and Rico here. Enjoying all that Bermuda offered. She knew he would love it. What's more, she would love to be here with him. Watching the sun rise and set with him would be so romantic. Enough of the daydreaming; it was time to return to her vacation with her girls. They were having the time of their lives. Bermuda was turning out to be one of their favorite places. There was so much beauty here. Tammy felt fortunate to visit such a beautiful place. When they were done shopping, they strolled down to the beach to enjoy a nice swim in the ocean. The weather was warm, with an island breeze flowing through the land. The water was blue, with plenty of white sand to get between their toes. Char got in the water first. In no time, there were dozens of people around her. Stephanie and Tammy just hung back to let her fans get time with her. Char loved her fans; she had no problem dealing with them like celebrities. She took pictures with them and signed autographs. She would do anything for her fans. They were everything to her. Deep down, Char knew she wouldn't be anything without her fans. The clothes, the locations, the glamor, the money. All that was great, but her fans kept her driven to be the best she could be. She wasn't one of those celebrities that took her fans for granted. She was one of those celebrities that celebrated her fans. She had come a long way in the modeling game; her fans had been there for her every step! Her life would be much different without them! Tammy and Stephanie got in the ocean when the crowd dispersed. "Wow, Char, does that happen everywhere that you go?" Stephanie asked. "Fortunately for me, it does." "Do you ever tire of dealing with strangers wanting to spend time with you?" Tammy asked. "Actually, not at all. I love dealing with my fans. I have the best fans in the world!" "Char, you truly love this life, don't you? You eat this stuff up." Stephanie said, "Yeah, I love it. I wouldn't trade it for a million dollars. This is all I have ever wanted to be since I was a little girl. I don't have to tell y'all that, though. Stephanie, I don't know where I would be now if it wasn't for your father. He helped me get started in all this."

"Yeah, sometimes my parents and I talk about the good ole days. That is always one of the biggest topics that come up. They truly love you, Char. They couldn't be happier for you either." "That's great because I truly love them too. You are so lucky to have them as parents. They are so supportive of all of us." "Yeah, they consider all of you as their children. I don't mind sharing them with y'all." "Good, 'cause it's not like you really have a choice. We all have been a family for years." "When my parents took a turn for the worst. Your parents stepped in and took care of everything. I agree with Char; I wouldn't be the person I am today had it not been for your parents." Tammy said. "Okay, ladies, enough of the reminiscing. Let's get to swimming while we still can." Char stated. They walked farther out in the water until they were waist-high. "Wait, ladies, what the hell are we doing? We can't go any farther. If we go swimming, we will mess up our hair. I am not trying to do my hair tonight." Tammy said. "You are so right; that would not be a good idea. Let's stay where we are." Char said. "Let's see if we can find something good to eat." Stephanie said. Tammy and Char burst into laughter. They both knew that it would only be a matter of time before Stephanie would bring up getting something to eat. In all actuality, the other girls were getting hungry too. Food would be a great idea right about now. Which was a good thing for Stephanie?

They found a nice local restaurant just up the boardwalk from them. When they walked in, the place was packed. That was a great sign; this place had great food. There was about a twenty-minute wait before they seated the ladies. Once seated, Stephanie immediately asked for the best dish on the menu. She figured, whatever it was, it had to be spectacular. Tammy and Char perused their menus to see if there was anything on there that would catch their attention. Stephanie was ready and willing to help with their decision on what to eat. The menu read like a foreign language to Char and Tammy. They had to look at the ingredients rather than the name of the meal. Stephanie found two meals she thought they both would love. She suggested to Tammy that the grouper dish would be a great choice for her. As for Char, she suggested that the fish chowder would be an excellent choice. They would all have the rum cake and some pepper jelly for dessert. When their meals arrived, they were steaming hot. The flavors that emitted from the dishes were divine. Stephanie enjoyed every single bite of her meal. Char and Tammy ate their meals and didn't really think much about it. To them, it was just food to feed their hunger. To Stephanie, it was much more. It was everything to her. Food was her life!

Chapter 17

Ingrid lay on the surgery table, still fighting for her life. The surgeon tried his best to save her. Although things looked bleak for her, time was of the essence. She was hanging on by a thread. The threat of death was imminent.

Cashmere, Uncle Herbert, and Damion didn't know that Ingrid was fighting for her life. All they knew was that the baby was born. They hadn't seen the baby yet. The nurses were still working on her. They would bring the baby in as soon as Ingrid returned from surgery. When that would be, it was anyone's guess.

Ingrid turned for the worse, and her blood pressure dropped significantly. Everyone was in panic mode. She was losing the battle of her life. Then it happened; her heart monitor went blank. The staff began CPR. They were trying to bring her back. Chest compressions, breath. More chest compressions, then another breath. They kept that rhythm up for three minutes before her heart beat again. "She's back, she's back!" shouted the nurse. "Okay, let's get her stabilized, stat!" The doctor said Ingrid's heart was beating, but it was faint. Her breathing was labored; she was far from out of the woods. This was a crucial time. The doctor knew he was working with a short window of opportunity.

Ingrid's heart could stop beating again at any moment. "Give her twenty to thirty mcg of inotropes by intravenous injection now. We have to increase the heart rate as soon as possible. It's our only chance to save her!" said the doctor. Ingrid was trying her best to fight. Her heart wasn't strong enough on its own. Her body was weakening, but not her spirit. Her spirit was still fighting; she would not give up. She couldn't give up. Now, the inotrope was flowing through her veins. Her heart was reacting slowly but surely to the medication. Ingrid's body was seizing. She was shaking wildly, foaming from the mouth. She was dying again. The drug wasn't working quick enough. "We're losing her! We're losing her!" The doctor screamed! The monitor went blank again. They started CPR once more. Chest compressions, breath. More chest compressions, another breath. They kept that rhythm up for twenty minutes until the doctor looked at the clock and said, "Time of death is six thirty-two pm."

"No, we can't give up." The nurse said. "We can't do any more for her now. I'm sorry, she's gone. I'll tell her family!" The doctor said sadly. The nurse pulled the sheets over Ingrid's face and walked out of the operating room. Tears rose in her eyes because she knew this young lady would never see her child. She could never hold her child; her child would never know her. Her child would grow up without her. It was hard losing patients in this career field. It was tough losing young mothers that hadn't had the chance to hold their newborn babies. Life could be so cruel sometimes. Now comes the even more challenging part. The doctor had to tell the family that their loved one didn't make it. That is the single worst thing that a doctor can say to anyone.

The baby was doing better. Its color was fair, lungs seemed to work okay. The baby had a good cry. It also went to the bathroom, which meant the plumbing was working. They had to keep her on oxygen and intravenous fluids to stabilize her so she would continue to live. She should be able to breathe independently in two weeks, and her weight should be adequate. This baby was a fighter, just like her mother was.

The doctor stood outside Ingrid's hospital room and took a deep breath to regain composure. He opened the door and stepped inside. As soon as he walked inside the room, all eyes were on him. The silence felt endless. It felt like years had passed before he uttered a word to break the silence. "The baby is in the NICU, there are complications, but nothing we can't take care of. You should be able to go see her shortly." "And Ingrid? How is Ingrid?" Cashmere asked. "Well, I am sorry. We tried everything we could, but Ingrid did not make it through this. She passed away at six thirty-two this evening. I truly am very sorry." Cashmere got up, walked over to the window, and looked out. "No, no! This can't be! Not my baby sister. Lord, why her? Why, her lord?" Cashmere burst into uncontrollable tears. Uncle Herbert went over to her, trying to console her. He became overwhelmed with tears too. Damion had a look of disbelief on his face; he sat in the chair as tears ran down his face. The three of them were facing their worst fears! Ingrid was gone. She had left them a bundle of joy, but she was gone, just the same. The nurses came into the room shortly after the doctor had left. "You can come over and meet the little one." One nurse said. The three of them followed the nurses to the NICU. "Okay, come on in, but please be careful. She has a lot of tubes hooked up to her." "Is she okay?" Damion asked. "Well, since she was born premature, we must take these precautions to ensure that she gets all the care and medication needed to get her through the next week." "When will we be able to hold her?" Cashmere asked. "Not for about a week. We must ensure she is responding well to the treatments first. I meant to ask you, what will be the child's name?" "Her name is Ingrid Cashmere Riggins. That's exactly what Ingrid wanted it to be." Uncle Herbert said. "Great, we will add Ingrid Cashmere Riggins to the documents." One nurse said. "Yes, please let me know what documents you need signatures on, and I will be glad to take care." Cashmere said. "Well, since the mother passed away, the father is the next in line to take care of all the legal paperwork." "The father?" "Yes, the father. Are one of you gentlemen the father of the baby?" "Yes, I am the father. She is so adorable. She looks just like Ingrid." Damion said. Cashmere gave Damion a snide look. She knew it was the right thing to do, but she still wasn't comfortable with the thought of Damion being around yet. She wasn't satisfied with him being the father of Ingrid's baby, her niece. She couldn't believe all the people in the world; Ingrid ended up with Damion. And her dying wish was for them to raise the baby together. To share parental rights and decisions for the next eighteen to twenty-one years. How was that going to work out for them? They both faced a very uncomfortable situation they would be a part of for a very long time. This would be hard for everyone involved, especially for little Ingrid. How would it affect her to know that her mother died while giving birth to her? Would she somehow, later in life, blame herself for that?

Chapter 18

After a fun-filled day in Barbados, the Diamond Line was setting sail to return to Cape Hatteras. The girls were more than ready to set sail. There was something about being on a ship late at night. The water was still and beautiful. Unless dolphins or whales were swimming alongside the boat. It was so great laying out on the lido deck, late at night, under the star-laced sky. It was something they had done every night of their trip so far. It would have been nice if Cashmere could have enjoyed this experience with them. That would have made it complete for everyone. It would have given them something to reminisce on. This whole trip was supposed to do that for the foursome. They would have to tell Cashmere about it when they returned to Virginia. They would fill her in on everything she missed. One thing is for sure, they missed her being with them. It was so unfortunate she had to leave. It was just as sad that Ingrid wasn't doing well. They had hoped that things would work out for them. That Ingrid and the baby would be well. If it didn't turn out that way, things would be for the worst. It would forever change their lives. It was time for the girls to get their dancing on at one of the ship's clubs. Tonight they would try out Rare Gems, a swanky, chic club that was definitely for the most affluent of sorts. The club boasted a well-stocked cigar bar. A fabulous seafood bar. There were three dance floors with three separate deejays. This place was phenomenal.

Rico's VIP service was still in effect. So, the girls had nothing to worry about. They brought out the usual to them as soon as they mentioned their names. Rico had pulled out all the stops. It may be a little late in their relationship, but Tammy wondered how Rico was so well off. They hadn't really talked about their financial situations. However, Rico knew how she earned her income. Rico worked at Layla's cafe and was part owner of The Crib. She wasn't sure how much money they made in a week or a month. One thing that she was sure about was that it wasn't enough for him to live the lifestyle he was living. So, he must have had money all along. Did he have an inheritance of some sort? Her curiosity was piqued now; she would have to find out. How would he react, though, if she asked him? Would he think she was intrusive, or would he share that information with her without issues?

While sipping on some Moscato, Tammy asked Char and Stephanie, "Where do you think Rico got all his money from?" "I don't have a clue, Tammy. Why are you asking, though?" Char said, "To be honest, I am not sure. It occurred that I don't know how he made his money." "Here's a question, does it really matter, Tammy?" Stephanie asked. "Well, not really. I guess I am just wondering why he's never discussed it." "He need not discuss where he made his money from. It shouldn't make a difference if he isn't doing anything illegal." Stephanie said. "I know it shouldn't make a difference, but I am curious." "How curious are you?" Char asked. "Wait, you're not thinking about asking him, are you?" Stephanie said. They both looked at Tammy. "Wait, you can't really be serious about asking him." Char said. "Why not?" "Well, I think it would just be rude. How would you feel if he asked you how you made your fortune?" Char said. "That's just it; he knows how I make my money, though." "How do you know that he didn't make his fortune from being a part owner of The Crib?" Stephanie asked. Tammy looked at Stephanie. "Come on now, Stephanie! I am sure the place does well, but it can't be his sole source of income." "Maybe you should ask him, especially if you are adamant about finding out." Char commented. "Suppose he gets offended or doesn't answer me? Then what?" "Well, then, you have opened a huge can of worms. It will probably cause a serious problem between you two. So, be certain you really want to know. Pick your battles." Stephanie said. "I know, I know. I really want to know, though. It will drive me crazy if I don't try to find out, at least." "Try to find out. What does that mean? Are you thinking about trying to find out without asking him?" Char asked. "How would you do that, Tammy?" Stephanie said. "Well, if I had to resort to snooping, then I would have to do just that." "Wow... you are truly a trip. You would risk your relationship with a man that has been nothing but good to you just to find out how he made his money?" Char asked. "I don't really see the importance of knowing where he got his money from." Stephanie said. "Okay, here's a question. Suppose he got his money sordidly. He realized that he was living wrong, turned his life around, and now is living legitimately. Would you leave him for it?" Stephanie asked. Tammy thought long and hard before she answered. When she finally answered, she said, "I am not sure. I guess it would depend on how bad or illegal it was. I mean, suppose he was a hired killer or a drug kingpin. How would it look for one of Richmond's most prominent lawyers to be romantically involved with someone of that character." "Well, you better not open that door if you want your relationship to survive. If you find out down the road he has criminal tendencies, you can always break it off. You can just say you knew nothing about it." Char said. "Or, I can find out now and save myself the trouble later." "Sometimes, I dislike the way you think, Tammy. Sometimes, it seems like you sabotage yourself. You need to leave this alone." Stephanie said. Char refilled their glasses, hoping it would prompt Tammy to change the subject. There were plenty of other things for them to talk about that wouldn't include her sabotaging her relationship with Rico. "What's the first thing you will do when we get back, Char?" Stephanie asked. "I think I will go to Croaker Spot in Petersburg to enjoy some fantastic fish." What about you guys? What are y'all going to do when you get back?" "Well, I will stop by and see my parents to make sure they are doing okay." "Okay, I am going to just relax out back with a glass of Moscato and maybe some strawberries." "That sounds like a plan, Tammy. I may be a little envious." Char said. "Yeah, I will take some much-needed time for myself. It's been a minute since I have had some time. I think everybody needs that once in a while." Tammy said with a smile. "You couldn't be more correct. We get so caught up in our busy lives that we forget or neglect to take time for ourselves." Char said. "Yeah, we all need to take time out for ourselves to de-stress." Stephanie said.

Tammy put a few chocolate-covered strawberries on her plate and refilled her wine glass. The music was very nice. Plenty of people were on the dance floor. It would have been lovely to dance. She was so engulfed in their conversation that she really hadn't paid attention to anything else. They hadn't even noticed the young men standing close to them, trying to get their attention. Neither of them wanted to tell the attention seekers they didn't have a chance. But that wasn't what this trip was about. This trip was about bonding with one another. Getting away from the hustle and bustle of everyday life, including the men in their lives. Although, it really hasn't worked out that way for Tammy so far. Her mind has been on Rico for the better part of the cruise. Stephanie had the unfortunate task of trying to keep her mind off him and on the cruise. This cruise turned out to be a wonderful experience.

Chapter 19

When Rico woke up Saturday morning, he felt like he had a bad dream. A dream that R.J. had done business with Funk, and now they were into him for twenty-five large. He realized it wasn't a dream when he saw a text from R.J.

R.J.... Yo, have you heard from Funk yet? We have until tomorrow to get them the money.

Rico... No, I haven't heard from him yet. I am sure he will get at me today.

R.J.... Man, I hope you are right. If you aren't, we are fucked.

Rico... Have a little faith, my brother. We will work it out. One way or another!

R.J.... All right, man, talk to you later.

Rico... All right, I'll see you soon.

Rico didn't really want to let on how worried he was. He didn't wish R.J. to freak out anymore than he already had. But unfortunately, he would have to go with his backup plan. So, he did the only thing he could think of to do. He called his uncle!

Crush... Hey Rico! How are you doing, nephew?

Rico... I could be better, Uncle Crush.

Crush... What do you mean? What's going on?

Rico... Okay, here goes. You remember R.J., right?

Crush... Yeah, what about him?

Rico... Well, he got involved with some bad cats. He's into them for twenty-five large.

Crush... Let me guess, he doesn't have all the money.

Rico... Exactly!

Crush... So, you need my services?

Rico... Yes! You know I wouldn't bother you unless it was severe. These dudes don't play!

Crush... How many cats are we talking about? Is it a couple, or is it a gang of fools?

Rico... Well, two primary cats need handling.

Crush... Dealt with? Be specific. What is it you want to happen to them? You know how I roll, so you better be sure!

Rico... I know unc. I need them to be gone.

Crush... As in no more?

Rico... Yes, uncle. As in no more.

Crush... Okay, say no more. I am on the next plane smoking. I'll see you tonight.

Rico... Okay, thanks, Crush!

When Rico hung up the phone, he almost regretted making the call to Crush. He knew Crush didn't play.

He made people disappear for a living. Crush would definitely ensure that Funk and Slick were not heard from again. His decision to call him was extreme, but sometimes situations need a drastic measure.

He showered and got dressed. Got in the ride and headed to The Crib to touch base with R.J. When he got there, R.J. was at the bar indulging in some gin and juice. "It's a little early to be doing that, isn't it?" "Well, to be honest, I need something to take my mind off this fiasco we are going through." "I feel you, but you must have your wits. You never know if Slick or Funk will show up today." "Why would they show up today? The deadline isn't until tomorrow." "Oh, you think we are dealing with professional businessmen? These fools don't care about a deadline. They could pop up anytime, and we need to be ready. Speaking of being ready, do you have a strap?" "A strap?" "Yeah, R.J., a strap. We will need firepower in case they come in here guns blazing." "Damn, I didn't think it would get that drastic. Yes, I have firepower in the ride." "Cool, get it and keep it near. You could need it."

R.J. poured himself another gin and juice. Things had just gone to the next level for him. It was way too real now. "Man, I will do nothing like this again if we make it through this alive." "I think it goes without saying. At least, I would hope so anyway!" R.J. couldn't believe he had jeopardized everything they had worked so hard for. Their lives had been successful up to this point. But, now, it could all be over.

Rico's phone rang. Looking at it, he saw that Funk was calling. "Shit, it's Funk. Hold on a minute."

Rico... Funk, what's up?

Funk... Rico, my man. What's going on?

Rico... You know what it is, Funk. Any good news?

Funk... I talked to him yesterday after I left the club.

Rico... And? Was he with it?

Funk... Man, at first, he was like, hell no! But, then, he said you fools should have known what you were getting into when you agreed.

Rico... Man, I wasn't even in on this. I had no clue!

Funk... Yeah, I explained that to him. I think that's what made him change his mind.

Rico... So, how many more days do we have?

Funk... He gave y'all until Monday night after the club closes.

Rico... Monday night. We need more time than that. We need at least until Tuesday.

Funk... Look, man, what the hell you want from me? This isn't a bank. Just have the money by Monday night!

Rico... I guess we don't have a choice then.

Funk... Oh, you have a choice. You can choose not to have the money, and Slick will handle his business!

Rico... I hear you, man. We'll get it taken care of. Thanks for talking to him.

Funk... It's all good, Rico. Rico?

Rico... What Funk?

Funk... No matter what, you are still my boy.

Rico... Man, I hope you remember that on Monday night!

Rico hung up the phone. He looked over at R.J. and said, "We are fucked! At the latest, we need to have the money by Monday night." "Monday night, how in the hell are we going to pull that off?" "I don't have a clue, but we better figure out something. We better figure it out fast!"

R.J. poured another gin and juice. This time he swigged it down like it was a shot. He looked at Rico. "You want one?" "No, I'm good, thanks." "Suit yourself; I will have another one." "Man, you need to slow down." "Yeah, I will do that right after I finish this one!" "R.J., maybe you should go back and sleep this off." "I'll be fine, don't worry about it."

Rico went behind the bar to take an inventory of what we may need for the night. He needed R.J. to get his mind together. He needed him to be on top of his game right now. Neither of them could get caught slipping. This wasn't the time for R.J. to be drinking heavily. Rico knew that R.J. was stressed. As soon as this shit was over, he would be back to normal or as close to it as possible. Once Rico finished the bar inventory, he went to the storeroom to pull what he needed. R.J. stayed at the bar, depleting the gin and juice.

Chapter 20

Cashmere had to deal with the unfortunate demise of her little sister. They left her in charge of taking care of her funeral arrangements and ensuring that little Ingrid was doing okay. Somehow, when it was time to take care of the fundamental issues, Damion had found time to excuse himself. He seemed to have disappeared for two hours. Something didn't seem right about his actions. Cashmere was frustrated with him but didn't have time to deal with it, at least not right now. She needed to ensure that Ingrid's funeral arrangements were in order and get tiny Ingrid home. Luckily, Uncle Herbert was still around to help as much as he could. It was indeed a heart-wrenching situation for everyone involved. It was the most traumatic ordeal that Cashmere and Uncle Herbert had to endure. They had lost people they were close to, but this was different. It was Ingrid! Her baby sister, his youngest niece. Ingrid had lost her life far too soon. But, she was living, just beginning to flourish. And now, she is gone.

"Why Uncle Herbert? Why did he take her so soon?" "Baby, I don't know. Maybe GOD needed her to do bigger and better things." "It's just not right. I can't believe that she's gone." Uncle Herbert went over to Cashmere to console her. "It will be okay. We will make sure she is well cared for. I know it's hard for you. It's hard for me too, baby!" "I know, Uncle Herbert, I know. I can't believe it, though." Cashmere wept. Her emotions had overwhelmed her; there wasn't any way she could hold back the tears anymore. She had to be vital for everyone, so she held back the tears. Now, they were running down her face like a waterfall. As much as she tried to hold them back, they kept flowing like an ever-flowing stream. How would she ever get through these funeral arrangements? She would have to find strength and some courage from somewhere to make it through.

"Ingrid passed away today!" Damion told Bree. "I'm sorry to hear that, Damion; how is the baby doing?" "My daughter Ingrid is alive but in a serious condition." "Well, why don't you come over later, and I'll help you get over this whole thing!" "What? Come over. Did you hear what I said?" "Yes, baby, I heard you. That's why I want to take care of you tonight. I know what you need to feel better!"

"Bree, I don't think I can deal with you tonight. I will talk to you tomorrow." Damion said right before he hung up the phone. "Damion? Damion?" Bree said before she realized that he had hung up. She called him back, but his phone just went straight to voicemail. Damion couldn't believe how insensitive she was being. He didn't have time to worry about Bree right now. Having to deal with the death of Ingrid and make sure his daughter was doing okay. Not to mention, he had to deal with Cashmere and Uncle Herbert. He was convinced that Cashmere would be gunning for him when he returned. He knew she already had mega issues with him, and his disappearance would only add to those issues. He was more than right. As soon as he entered the hospital room, Cashmere lit into him with the quickness. "Where in the hell have you been? If this is any sign of how responsible you will be going forward, we may as well sever this deal right now!" "First, Cashmere, I am a grown-ass man, and I won't have you talking to me as if I am a child. You need to get your act together if this will work out!" Uncle Herbert looked at Cashmere. They were both thinking the same thing. Did he talk to her like that? Cashmere walked over to Damion, looked him square in his eyes, and said, "I am not sure who the hell you think you are talking to, but it surely isn't me. Think more clearly about the things you say going forward. That is your only warning!"

"Warning, you think a lot of yourself, don't you? You may scare your friends, you may even have scared Ingrid, but you don't scare me, Cashmere. You can talk all that ish to someone else!" She rolled her eyes at Damion and said, "Is that so?" "Yes, Cashmere, it is so. Ain't nobody worried about you!" "I tell you what, Damion, you better be worried about me. You are on a thin line with me. Please believe you don't want to see me angry with you." "Please believe I don't want to see you at all. Unfortunately, I have little choice in the matter. Let's get another thing straight while we are at it. The baby, your sister, had is mine. I am the parent, not you. She may have wanted you to help raise her, but I have the final say as the father. You can cross me, but I'll ensure you don't see *my child.* So, if I were you, I would play nice in the sandbox!" Silence befell the room; it shocked uncle, Herbert. He had heard nobody talk to Cashmere that way. At least, not as an adult! Cashmere looked at Damion with disbelief. She had to save face, so she uttered a comeback. "Oh, I see. You think you are talking to some weak woman. Let me break this down for you so you can understand it. You can talk about all that stuff if you want; you can't defeat me. Damion, you don't have it in you. You didn't have it when we were in high school, and you still don't have it in you now. So, please understand, when it comes to me, you don't have a clue just how far I will go to prove how little you mean to me." "Whatever, Cashmere! We'll see about all that noise you're talking about." Without a chance to respond, he stepped around her and headed to the door.

"Uh, I can't stand him. He gets on my last nerve. Please, Lord, keep me from killing that fool!" Cashmere shouted. "Well, Cashmere, he has a point. He is the father, and you should treat him with respect; he is the man that Ingrid chose to have a child with." "Uncle Herbert, whose side are you on? Ingrid didn't choose to have a child with him. She, unfortunately, got pregnant by him. Unfortunately, she's gone, and we must deal with this foul individual." "Baby, I am not taking anybody's side. I know Ingrid wouldn't want you two at each other's throats. So, please try to be a little more open to what he is going through for her sake. He is a father now, and I am sure he doesn't know how to raise this child." "I hear you, Uncle Herbert, but I am not ready to deal with his foolishness." "Unfortunately, you don't have any choice. It is just going to be very hard for me to deal with. I'm not too fond of Damion. He is less than human. Had I known she was seeing him, I would have made her end it before any of this happened." "Made her put an end to it. Yes, she was your little sister, but she was an adult. You can't make anybody do anything. You can give your opinion, and that's it." "And that's your opinion!"

"Why don't you like him? Did he do something to you to make you not like him?" Cashmere got quiet; she walked over to the window, pretending to look out. The truth was she didn't want to answer the question. "Well, Cashmere?" "Uncle Herbert, I would rather not talk about it now." "When will you feel like talking about it? Is it something I should know about?" "I don't know! When I am ready to talk about it, I will!" She kept looking out the window, trying to hide the tears rolling down her face.

Chapter 21

They were down to their last night on the cruise line; it would dock in Cape Hatteras in the morning. The cruise was ending. Even though Cashmere had to leave the cruise, they tried to make the best of it. Once Char arrived, it made it a lot easier to enjoy. Tomorrow, they had to pick up the rental car and head back to Virginia to resume their everyday lives. They also had to find out about Ingrid and the baby since neither of them had spoken to Cashmere in several days. Partly because they weren't sure what she would say about Ingrid, all they knew was that they didn't want to hear any bad news. All they wanted to hear was that Ingrid and the baby were doing well.

For the last night on the ship, Char pulled out all the stops. She talked the captain into letting her organize a party for all aboard. The theme would be "Come As

You Are." The captain was a little hesitant at first. He thought that would attract an element he wasn't sure was appropriate for the cruisegoers to participate in. But, Char convinced him it would be the party of all times. It would be something that wouldn't be soon forgotten for a while to come. She also said she would cover the expenses for the evening. That seemed to get his attention more than anything else she had said.

We all know that the bottom line is money. Money makes the world go round, making the ship's captain reconsider his decision. He quickly agreed with one condition. That was that Char would sit beside him at his table tonight. Char promptly declined his offer with good reason. She told him that if she sat at his table, she wouldn't be able to access her fans. She needed them to be able to come to her if they wanted to speak with her. The captain contemplated a rebuttal but realized it wouldn't make a difference. Since she was footing the bill, she would have the final say where she sat. The captain agreed reluctantly as he slowly walked in another direction. Char was happy that she didn't have to continue debating with him. While his efforts were admirable, she felt the captain had another plan. A plan she didn't want to be a part of. So, rather than hurt his feelings later, she diffused the situation before it escalated. She had a way of reading people, a form of reading men. The captain had been friendly enough to accommodate several of her requests. She didn't want to cause an issue with him. One never knows when you will need a favor. Char was not one to burn bridges if she could help it. The night had arrived, and Char and the girls had made their way to the club. The deejay was spinning some funky grooves. Partygoers were in the place, drinks flowing, people dancing. The party was happening.

Char entered and strolled over to the VIP area. All eyes were on her as she sat, looking as stunning as ever! Tammy and Stephanie were looking as magnificent as ever. Autograph seekers stare to get a glimpse of Char, the supermodel. She greeted every fan as if they were a friend. She gladly signed all autographs and took many pictures. Once the line depleted, she went to the dance floor and got her groove on. Tammy and Stephanie were right there with her. A few of her fans surrounded them. They were dancing around them, having a grand ole time. The night was in full effect. Tammy and Stephanie couldn't stop smiling. They were having the time of their lives. Char knew how to bring the best out in people. She had a knack for getting people to come together. What better way to do so than to have an end-of-cruise celebration? People were partying together, getting to know one another. Friendships crafted. Memories made. Char was on the stage with the mic in hand. She was ready to make an announcement.

"Excuse me, everybody. I wanted to thank everybody for coming out tonight. I hope you are having a great time! I want to thank Captain Henderson for allowing us to come together like this on the last night of the cruise. Everybody, please give him a round of applause." Captain Henderson stood up, smiled, and waved to the crowd. "Also, I wanted you all to know that I am launching my clothing line. You can purchase it at your local stores. Please look for From My Mother's Closet clothing line as early as January 2019. Thanks for supporting me throughout my modeling career. I hope that you continue to support me with my clothing line. Okay, enough of the business. Let's get back to partying. Deejay, crank that beat right now!"

Char stepped off the stage, went straight to the dance floor, and resumed dancing with her girls. People were throwing their hands in the air, getting their fun on. Captain Henderson came up to Char and danced with them. "Char, thank you so much for organizing this event. Just as you said it would be, it is something to remember for some time." "You are welcome. I am glad it worked out for everyone. Everyone seems to have a great time. I know I am." She smiled at Captain Henderson as he mingled with some other partygoers. This was a great night! Many people were reluctant to leave the party when the night was over. They wanted it to continue. They tried to keep on dancing and drinking. People lingered as long as they could to be sure they missed nothing. Char, Tammy, and Stephanie finally ended up leaving. When Tammy looked back, there was a crowd of people following them. Following Char, to be exact. The girls walked at a quicker pace to try to lose the followers. Unfortunately, it didn't work. When they got to their room, some came down the hall. They quickly entered their stateroom and locked the door. Stephanie peered through the peephole and saw a crowd hanging out in the hallway. "Char, you have got to see this. There must be fifteen people outside the door. This is crazy!" "It is not crazy. It is the norm. Usually, there are quite a few more. Security always has to come and make them leave. I hate that part, but I can't do anything about it." "Damn girl, I'm not sure I could get used to something like that," Tammy said. "I never get used to it. It seems like the first time, every time. I am just grateful that they love me." "Char, you are fortunate to have a career like this. I know quite a few people that would kill to have your career." Tammy stated. "I am fortunate and blessed. I take none for granted. I know these blessings can be taken away tomorrow. That's why I try giving my fans as much of myself as possible." "You are probably the most humble person I know. It is amazing." Stephanie said. "That's why her fans love her so much. They know that she cares about them." Tammy said. "Thank you, Tammy; I try to treat them like the fans they are."

Chapter 22

Rico's phone rang.

Rico... Hey, Uncle Crush. Are you here?

Crush... Yeah, my plane just landed. Are you at the airport yet?

Rico... Yeah, I'm here at baggage claim.

Crush... Cool, give me about ten minutes, and I will be out there.

Rico... Great, I can't wait to see you, Uncle Crush. It's been a minute.

Crush... Yeah, me too. It has been a while. I am getting off the plane now.

Rico... Cool, I'll be waiting for you at baggage claim seven.

Crush... All right, should be there in a bit.

Crush walked up and smacked Rico on the back of the head.

Rico... What the hell?????

Rico turned around to see Crush standing right there.

Crush... What's going on, nephew? How have you been?

Rico... Man, don't hit me in the back of my head like that!

Crush... Man, you better watch who you talk to like that. I'll bust you up right here!

Rico... Man, you are always talking shit. You better watch that. Things have changed since you last saw me. I'm not that little boy anymore!

Crush... Is that supposed to mean something? Boy, I whipped your ass then, and I will destroy your ass now!

Rico looked at his Uncle Crush, and they both burst into laughter.

Rico... Man, you always got some funny shit going on.

Crush... You know how I do.

Rico... Let's get your bags and get this party started.

Crush... Cool; I see one of them coming now. Also, I sent something to your crib. Did you get it?

Rico... Yeah, it came this morning.

Crush... Cool. All right, let's get out of here.

Crush picked up his bags, and they headed to the car. Laughing and joking all the way. It had been many years since they had seen one another. Crush had always been a little on the sketchy side of the family. They were never sure of what he could do. After someone murdered his father, he seemed to get worse. He didn't give a damn about anybody after that. He ran with the wrong crowd and did all kinds of crazy things. His father's death hit him hard. It was like he became worse. Almost as if he thought he was above the law. He was definitely missing his dad. He was missing a vital part of who he was. His mother was still a great parent, and she immediately tried to fill the void, but she couldn't teach him the things his father could. There's a special bond between a father and son that a mother just can't fulfill. Crush had lost that bond with his father. What's more, he had lost his father forever!

Crush... Tell me about these cats you need me to deal with.

Rico... They are some bad dudes. R.J. is into them for 25 large, and we don't exactly have all of it.

Crush... What type of skills do they possess?

Rico... Funk is more or less the spokesperson for the group. Slick is the enforcer and is well trained in combat and weaponry.

Crush... Oh, so Slick is the one I must take out first? Funk will fall after that.

Rico... Yeah, Slick is the real issue. He is the firepower.

Crush... How many others are there in the crew?

Rico... There are about ten others, but they won't be a problem once you take out Slick. Slick is the ringleader.

Crush... Okay, cool. Can we go by the club, so I can get the layout down? I need to find the best vantage point to take Slick out.

Rico... Yeah, no doubt.

Crush... Okay, cool.

Rico... We can roll by there tonight.

Crush... That would be best. Could you drop me off at the Hyatt after that?

Rico... But you know you can stay with me.

Crush... Yeah, but I don't want to bring any attention to your crib. When all of this goes down, you can't have any connections with me. So if this goes as I think it will, it will be paramount.

Rico... I understand, but if it is done at the club, it will come back anyway. Isn't that right?

Crush... Well, maybe, I can get them before they enter the club.

Rico... What do you mean?

Crush... I mean, maybe I can get them while they are driving up the street, instead of when they enter the club.

Rico... Like that, Unc?

Crush... Most definitely. I don't play when it comes to getting it done! I need to know what kind of car they drive and when they are due to arrive.

Rico... I'll get you all that information.

Crush... Cool!

Rico knew that he had made the right choice, calling Crush. Unfortunately, when this was all over, Funk would be done for. There wasn't any genuine concern for Slick. Slick was notorious for making fools out of people. He didn't give a damn about anybody. If he was after you, you were as good as dead. It wasn't if it would happen; it was more like when. Crush was the perfect person for this situation. He would ensure that Funk and Slick would end up breathless!

Chapter 23

Cashmere lay in her bed, trying to stop the tears from rolling down her face. She tried to wish all that had happened away. No matter how hard she tried, she couldn't alter what had happened. Her baby sister was gone, and her niece was lying in the NICU, fighting for her life. Total sadness engulfed her; it destroyed her heart when her sister passed. Cashmere and Damion had arrangements to make for little Ingrid. It would forever change their lives; Little Ingrid would never know her mother. She would never get to hear her voice, ever! One thing is sure: Cashmere would ensure that little Ingrid knew all about her mother. She would make sure she knew just how special her mother was. Cashmere would assume her caregiver role but would make damn sure that little Ingrid knew just who her mother was. She told her sister she would help raise her child, and that's just what she intended to do. No matter how hard it would be, she would ensure that little Ingrid had the best life she could give her.

Little Ingrid lay in her hospital crib. Breathing on her own. After removing the intravenous tubes, she was doing well. She had overcome the first great fight of her life. Little Ingrid had persevered; she had beat the odds against her. Damian peered through the NICU window and smiled eased between his lips. His daughter was doing well. She had gotten through her darkest hours if only Ingrid were around to see it. From a distance came a voice. "How is she?" Uncle Herbert said as he walked up next to him. Damian looked at him with a huge smile, "She is doing well. She is breathing on her own. They took her IV out a few minutes ago. I couldn't be happier." "That's great. My great niece is doing her thing. She is a fighter, just like her mother!"

Uncle Herbert and Damian high-fived as Cashmere walked up. "My, aren't we so friendly?" She said with a smirk on her face. "Hello Cashmere, I see you woke up on the wrong side of the bed again," Damian said. Cashmere rolled her eyes at Damian, trying to dismiss his statement. "Hello, Uncle Herbert; how are you today?" "It is a joyous day, baby girl. She is breathing independently, and they have taken the IV out. Little Ingrid is getting better. We will take her home soon." "Praise GOD, she will make it out of this. She will really get better."

Cashmere hugged Uncle Herbert. Uncle Herbert motioned for Damian to join them. Damian was hesitant because he knew Cashmere would object. He leaned and put his arms around them. She looked at Damian. Much to everybody's surprise, especially Damian's, she continued to hug them. Maybe this was part of Ingrid's plan all along. Could it be that she knew about the heart issue she knew that Cashmere and Damian had dated? Could this have been a ploy to get them together again? Why would she risk it all for them, though? Why would she give her life for it? Why????? If this was, in fact, her plan, no one could answer those questions. She would be the only one with the answers. Unfortunately, she wouldn't be able to tell anyone her reasons. Whatever they were, they must have been significant to her. So important that it was worth her existence.

When Damian finished hugging them, he excused himself and went back to the window to look at Little Ingrid. She was crying; something had upset her. Damian went into the NICU to check on her. "What is wrong with her?" He asked the nurse. "She is hungry. We were just about to feed her." Damian looked at the nurse and questioned, "May I feed her, please?" "You may feed her.

I am sure she would like that very much. Here is her bottle." Damian took the bottle of Similac and held her in his arms. He couldn't help but smile as he fed his newborn daughter. She received the bottle and ceased her crying. A slight smile crossed her face, and that's when Damian fell madly in love with her. He couldn't stop smiling. His heart overflowed with elation. Cashmere peered through the window at Damian feeding her. If her eyes were fire, she would have burned a hole in the back of his head. In her mind, she should be the one feeding little Ingrid. After all, Ingrid was her sister. She walked towards the entrance of the NICU. "Cashmere, let him have time with his daughter." Uncle Herbert stated. She turned to look at Uncle Herbert, walking back to him. She reluctantly said, "I guess you're right. Little Ingrid and I will have plenty of time together." Although it pained her to see Damian with her sister's child, she knew that Uncle Herbert was right. Uncle Herbert was always right. "I will be back soon. I think I want to get coffee." Cashmere said before she turned and walked away. Uncle Herbert didn't speak; he kept watching Damian feed little Ingrid. He knew Cashmere hated Damian. She hated seeing little Ingrid smiling at him. This was part of Ingrid's wishes. Even though they didn't care for Damian, they had to respect Ingrid's wishes. Uncle Herbert had made peace with Ingrid's wishes and embraced them. He knew Cashmere wasn't there yet. It would take her some time to get there. Her hatred for Damian would cloud her judgment for doing the right thing. Hopefully, her love for Ingrid would help uncloud that.

Uncle Herbert walked into the NICU to be with Damian and little Ingrid. "She is amazing. So precious and beautiful! I can't believe she is my seed." Damian said. Uncle Herbert looked him dead in the eyes and said, "Damian, you are right. She is amazing, precious, and beautiful. But, please remember, just as much as she is your daughter, she is my niece's daughter." Damian looked at Uncle Herbert and said, "What is that supposed to mean?" "That means if you ever mistreat her or harm her. I will make sure you don't do it again!" Damian looked at Uncle Herbert with a smirk and said, "Old man, I will not even honor your insult with a reply. There isn't any fear here. I hope you understand that!" He looked down at little Ingrid and continued to feed her as Uncle Herbert turned and walked out. Damian couldn't believe that Uncle Herbert had come at him like that. He expected that from Cashmere but not from him. He thought Uncle Herbert was the smarter of the two. It wasn't the first time that Damian had been mistaken.

One thing was for sure, he knew he had to watch his back with them! They both would wait for him to mess up, waiting for an opportunity to swoop in and take little Ingrid from him. "Baby, I am your father and will do everything I can to ensure you are loved. To make sure you have the greatest life possible. Know that I will love you with all of my beings. I will love and care for you for as long as the breath flows through my body." The sight of his child had changed Damian. It had awakened something inside him he was unaware he had. Damian was now a father, and his daughter had his heart!

Chapter 24

When the Diamond line arrived in Cape Hatteras the following day. The girls disembarked the vessel that had been their home for the last nine days. They had enjoyed themselves as much as they could. It would have been much better if Cashmere had stayed. They had to get back to Virginia to check on Ingrid and Cashmere. "What shall we do now?" Char asked. "Breakfast would be nice. Let's see if we can find a nice place to eat." "I should have known, you would say that, Stephanie. You are always thinking about food." Tammy said. ". It is my career. Hell, it is my life. The cuisine has gotten me through some challenging times." "Cuisine... really, Stephanie? You are with your girls, you don't have to speak all restauranteur to us. We're your girls. We've known you forever. You can say food to us." Tammy said as she laughed. "Cuisine, really?" Tammy said under her breath. "Okay, okay. Food has gotten me through some challenging times. Is that better?" Stephanie said with a smile. "Yeah, that's better. We are on vacation, for goodness' sake. When you get back to work, you can speak to your staff like that." Char said. "Technically, our vacation is over since the cruise is over," Stephanie commented. "Technically, we aren't back in Virginia yet, so our vacation hasn't ended yet," Tammy said. "Whatever, ladies... can we enjoy what is left of our vacation?" Char said. "See Stephanie, she agrees with me," Tammy said. "Yeah, Tammy, way to be childlike!" Stephanie stated. "Ladies, let's get something to eat, then we can talk about going home," Char said, trying to end this craziness. "I am in total agreement," Tammy said. "Let's walk around the boardwalk and see what this city offers regarding tasty cuisine?" Char said. "Sounds like a plan. Let's do it." Stephanie said.

The ladies walked the boardwalk, where many people checked out all the touristy items for sale. Finally, they stumbled upon a store with all kinds of little knick-knacks for sale. One thing that Tammy loved was knick-knacks. She could purchase many trinkets for her home and her loved ones. She walked in, and the ladies followed reluctantly. They knew how Tammy was when it came to her souvenirs or knick-knacks. She could spend hours in this store. "Oh my, I could really use something to eat," Stephanie said as she winked at Char. "You know what,

I could eat," Char said. Tammy ignored them and kept browsing for anything that would catch her eye in the store. She would not let them rain on her parade. There would be plenty of time to get something to eat. They would just have to indulge her at this point. She had submitted to both of them so many times before. Now, it was their turn to be indulgent! Tammy could tell that something bothered them, but she didn't give a damn. She was in her happy place. There were so many things in the store she wanted to purchase that it was hard for her to decide. She kept walking through the aisles, checking out the shelves. There were so many things she wanted to purchase, but she knew that wasn't smart. One of her weaknesses was spending money unnecessarily. She had controlled it ever since she met Rico. Unfortunately, she wasn't with Rico now, and her desire to spend money was kicking in overwhelmingly.

Stephanie and Char could not keep her from the desire to shop that was raging inside of her. Char walked next to her "Hey girl... how are you doing?" Tammy looked at her and said, "I am well, having a great time checking out the store. You Char?" She knew Char was only asking to get her out of the store. She wasn't taking the bait, though. She was determined to ensure that she enjoyed her shopping experience. It really didn't matter what they thought. This part of the vacation would be about her, and she would make sure of it too! Char was used to having things her way. She didn't have to worry about people challenging her status, but today, she would have to deal with that. Tammy was sure Char wouldn't like the response but wouldn't have a choice but to deal with it. Tammy was not one of her super fine model flunkies; she was one of her best friends. This was their everyday life and not the glamorous runway life! Char would just have to get over it and endure the realities of sisterhood as far as Tammy was concerned.

I'm looking forward to getting home. I'm looking forward to getting some much-needed rest."

Tammy saw the perfect diamond bracelet; she had to have it. It had been a time since she had splurged on herself. Today would be the day she made up for it. She loved the way the diamonds sparkled around her wrist. It was stunning. "That is a beautiful bracelet. It looks fantastic on you." Char said with a smile. She knew that saying anything else would not be an intelligent thing to do. After leaving the store, Stephanie wanted to get something to eat. Char was eager to get home, so she suggested they charter a jet to take them back to Virginia. It would be her treat. Stephanie and Tammy couldn't resist her offer.

When the plane was safely in the air, someone gave them filet mignon, asparagus, and creamy risotto to enjoy on their two-hour flight home. In two hours, they would be back on Virginia soil. A much-needed return for them all. Although the vacation was excellent, they all missed being home. They missed Cashmere. It was time to find out what was truly going on with Ingrid. It had been a time since either of them had heard from Cashmere. Neither of them had reached out to her either. They will talk to her tomorrow. Then, things would be back to normal for all of them. They would reach out to Cashmere and catch up on lost time.

When the jet landed at the airport, the ladies got in the limo Char had waiting for them. The limo would take Stephanie home first since she lived the closest. Once they arrived at Stephanie's place, she hugged Char and Tammy before she got out of the limo. The driver popped the trunk, gathered her bags, and took them to her front door for her. Stephanie waved to them as she entered her place. The limo pulled off, heading to Tammy's place next. Char and Tammy enjoyed a glass of Moscato on their way to her home. She took the time to tell Tammy that she enjoyed meeting them on the trip. It seemed to be precisely what she needed. When they pulled up to Tammy's, the driver opened her door and helped her with her bags. She hugged

Char before leaving the limo. Tammy entered her place just as the limo was pulling off. Char poured another glass of Moscato while waiting for the driver to pull up to her home. By the time she arrived, she had finished her wine. The driver opened her door, gathered her bags from the trunk, and walked her to the door. Char waved to the driver as he walked back to the limo. The driver pulled off as she closed the door. Char was back home. She was where she wanted to be. Her home was her sanctuary. She was most comfortable there. She placed her bags in the closet, went to her bathroom, and ran the bathwater. All she wanted now was to relax in the tub with some bubbles. Her day had been long. Her desire to be back at her place had heightened. She let the warm bubbles massage her body as she eased into her jacuzzi-sized tub. The water soothed her to the point of sheer relaxation. This was her time. Her time to just be plain ole Char. No glamor, no glitz, no frills. Just Char! She laid her head back on the tub and let the bubbles work their magic all over her body. When she finished, she toweled dry, went to her room, and fell on the bed. She lay there with a clear mind, enjoying her bed's comforts and solitude. Before she knew it, her eyes had closed, and she had fallen asleep. By the time she awoke, two hours had gone by. She got up and went to the kitchen to eat something. After that, she would unpack her bags and put her clothes away.

Chapter 25

When Rico showed up at the club, R.J. was by the sound booth, checking out the system. There had been issues with one speaker. He wanted to get it taken care of before the D.J. showed up. Rico walked over to R.J. and gave him some dap. "What's going on, young man?" "Just checking the equipment to make sure we are ready for tonight. What's up with you, Rico?" "Just stopping in to check on things. Funk and Slick will come for their money tonight. First, we must ensure that everything is complete for Crush." "Yeah, I know. I have been thinking about it all day. We need this to go off without a hitch. Are you sure that Crush can handle it?" "Yeah, I am sure. He should be here soon to check out the place. Don't worry; Crush knows exactly what he is doing." "Okay, Rico. I trust you, man!" "Cool, and I trust Crush."

"Hey, what do I have to do to get a drink in this place?" Speak of the devil, Crush just walked in. "What's up, Crush? How are you doing?" Rico asked. "I'm good, nephew. Things are well. Now, about that drink." "Yeah, no problem, come over here. Whatever you want is on the house." R.J. said. "I figured that it would be." I'll have a vodka and cranberry juice." Crush said with a smile. After getting his drink, he walked around the club, checking out the layout. He needed to find the best spot to take care of Funk and Slick. He walked into the office; R.J. and Rico were right behind him. "Okay, so here is the deal. Do you think you can get them to come to the office with you?" Crush asked. "I believe so, but it might be a little tricky. They may suspect something." R.J. said. "Well, if we tell them we want to take care of business privately, they may go for it. One question though, this office is small. How will you kill them without them seeing you?" Rico asked. "Okay, here is my plan. You see that window over there if you make sure it is open, with them standing in front. I can shoot them both through it." "How will you get both of them, though?" R.J. asked. "I will get Slick first, then shoot Funk right after. It shouldn't be an issue." "Where will you be when you do it?" "I will be across the alley, posted up in that building. It will be over before you know it. What time do you expect them to get here?" "They should be here at eight to set up." "Okay, so when they get here, have them come straight back here, and we will take them out." "What about the mess and the bodies? How will we deal with that?" Rico said. "Do you know of a cleaner?" "A cleaner?" R.J. questioned. "Yeah, someone that will come in and clean up the mess and get rid of the bodies." "Man, you know we don't roll with people like that. We aren't about that life. Not anymore anyway!" Rico stated. "We don't need this coming back on us either. We don't want to be connected with any of this." R.J. said. "That is the point. We will work something out with the cleaner. Let me make two phone calls. I'm sure I can come up with something." Crush took out his phone and dialed a number.

Crush... Hey, I need the number of a cleaning service in Richmond, VA. Do you know of anybody?"

Solo... I think I know of two people that can get it done. When do you need it done, and how many rooms are we talking about?

Crush... I need them for tonight, around 8:15. There should be two rooms.

Solo... Okay, let me work on it, and I will get back to you; or do you want me to have them call you?

Crush... Have them call me, so I can give them any other details they might need.

Solo... Okay, cool. I will give them your number.

Crush... Okay, thanks, Solo. I owe you one.

Solo... No, my brother, you owe me more than one. We will settle up when you return.

Crush... I hear you. I'll see you soon.

"Okay, we got the hookup on the cleaner now. My boy Solo will take care of it for us. We should receive a call soon to complete all the details." Crush said. "That's good. Hopefully, it will all be good." R.J. said. "I want this all to be over. We don't need this hanging over our heads any longer." Rico said. "Either way, you won't have to deal with Funk and Slick any longer. How will you handle the club tonight as far as music?" Crush asked. "Well, if need be, we can deejay tonight. Or we can just play music and not really have a deejay. We'll have it covered, don't worry about it." R.J. answered. "Great, it's almost seven. They will be here in an hour. What do we need to do to get ready for them?" Rico asked. "Well, I need to get my supplies out of the car. I also need to see if I can gain access to that building over there." Crush went out to the car to get his supplies. He walked over to the building and noticed a door. He picked the lock to gain access. He went up the stairs to find a vantage point in the building. He noticed a window. Looking out the window, he could see right into the club's office. He had found the perfect spot to take care of Funk and Slick. Crush was setting up his supplies when his phone vibrated.

Crush... Hello.

Nestor... Is this Crush?

Crush... Yes, this is Crush. Who is this?

Nestor... Crush, this is Nestor; you were referred to me because you need a cleaning service.

Crush... Yes, I do. Can you start tonight?

Nestor... Yes, we can. Please advise the address and time you need the service. Also, how many rooms will we need to clean?

Crush... Okay, I will forward the address over to you. We need two rooms cleaned at 8:15 sharp.

Nestor... Okay, sounds good. We will expect the address and arrive promptly at 8:15.

Crush... Great, see you then.

Crush ended the call and continued to get his supplies ready. He texts the address to Nestor. Everything was just about set. All he needed was for Funk and Slick to show up. He knew that they would be on time. They wanted their money, so they wouldn't be a minute late. Crush was all set up. He had the sniper rifle ready. When the time came, he would end them.

Just like clockwork, Funk and Slick had arrived on time. Slick strolled in with much attitude, staring at Rico and R.J. with fire in his eyes. He hoped that they didn't have the money. He was itching to spill blood tonight. "Yo, R.J., can we handle business or what?" Slick shouted. Rico looked at R.J. and nodded his head. "Yeah, man, come back to the office, and we can take care of that," R.J. said. Slick and Funk followed R.J. back to the office; Rico was right behind Funk. When they entered the office, Rico shut the door.

"All right, fool, where the hell is my money? You better have all of..." A bullet pierced the window before Slick could get the last word out. He dropped to the ground like a heavy stone. Funk looked over at Slick just before his body hit the ground. He turned to R.J. "What the hell is going on, R.J.?" Funk asked as he pulled out two desert eagles. "I thought we were boys!" Funk said as he was aiming the guns at Rico and R.J. Before he could squeeze the triggers, two more bullets pierced the window, and Funk flew backward, hitting the desk. His lifeless body rolled off the desk onto the floor. Rico looked down at both of them lying dead on the floor. He felt a rush of relief compiled with extreme nervousness. R.J. stared at the bodies, unsure what to say or do next. Then, there was a knock at the office door. "Yes, who is it?" Rico said with a slight shakiness in his voice. "Rico, there is someone here to see you. He said you are expecting them." One of the staff members said. "Okay, I will be right there. Thank you, you can return to work now." Rico said. He deliberately paused to give them time to walk away before walking to the door. Rico opened the door slowly, peeking around the corner to ensure no one was directly in front. He saw a man he didn't know. Assuming it was Nestor, he motioned for him to come closer. "Nestor, I presume." He said. "Correct, I am Nestor. Rico, I presume?" "Correct, please come in, Nestor."

Rico opened the door slightly to let Nestor in. Once Nestor was in the room, he immediately took notice of the two bloody bodies. He looked around the room for a splattering of blood and body tissue. "So, are these the only two rooms that need cleaning?" R.J. looked at

Nestor with a puzzled look on his face. "Yes, these are the only two rooms," Rico said. "Great, where does that door lead to?" "This door leads to the alley," R.J. said. "Great, we can gain access from there. Please wait a few minutes. I will go get my van and my guys. We will knock on this door in a few minutes. Let no one in here whatever you do until I return." Nestor said. Nestor pulled out his phone and exited the door leading to the alley. A few minutes later, he knocked on the door. When R.J. opened it, Nestor and four muscle-bound guys came in with him. "Okay, here are the rooms that need cleaning; get them taken care of ASAP. We also have walls to scrub and some stains on the desk and carpet. Get rid of anything that isn't important. I don't have to tell you that time is of the essence. Let's get it done, fellas!" The men took care of the bodies first. They put them in body bags and wrapped them in carpeting. After taking the bodies to the van, they came back in to start on the office. After wiping everything down, they went to the van and waited for Nestor. "Okay, we are all done here. Where is Crush?" Crush entered the office from the alley. "I am Crush." "Crush, Nestor here. I believe we spoke on the phone." "Yes, we did. It looks like you've done a great job. The place looks great. I appreciate your services." "We must settle up. Do I do that with you, or will Solo take care of everything?" "How much are we talking?" "Well, the bill is twenty large." "Twenty large, okay. I will take care of it." Crush opened his bag and pulled out twenty grand. "Here, this should take care of it." "A pleasure doing business with you. If you need my services again, you know how to reach me." Nestor said right before he left!

Crush looked around the room. Very pleased with the cleaners' work. "Crush, that was amazing. The way you took them both out. For a minute, I was nervous, but you were on point." R.J. said. "Did you expect anything less?" "Sorry, I have witnessed nothing like that before. I am a little surprised at how easily and quickly it all happened. Thank you so much for taking care of this for us! You saved our lives!" Rico looked at Crush because he knew Crush had just paid twenty grand to the cleaner. He would want his money back soon. Rico knew precisely what was getting ready to happen. He had seen it too many times before. "Okay, fellas, I have taken care of your little problem. However, there remains an issue we need to discuss." R.J. looked at Crush, wondering what he was talking about. "I know, Crush, we now owe you twenty grand." "What? Do we owe him twenty grand? We are right back where we started. How in the hell are we going to pay him twenty grand?" "Calm down, R.J., we will work this out," Rico said while looking at Crush. "Don't worry, I am not expecting the money right away.

You have one year from this day to pay it off." "And if we can't pay it off by then?"

R.J. asked. "If you can't pay it off by then, you must work off the remaining debt." "Work it off. What are you talking about, Crush?" R.J. asked. "Rico, tell your boy what I mean by that" Rico looked at R.J. and said, "He means we will have to get our hands dirty." "Oh shit. You mean you want us to take people out?" "Now, you're getting it. That's exactly what I mean. I do a favor for you, and you return favors for me." "We'll get you your money. Don't worry about that! Because I'm not killing anybody!" R.J. said.

Chapter 26

Cashmere completed the paperwork for her little sister's funeral arrangements. Now she had to wait for that dreaded day when they would lay her sister to rest. She couldn't help but cry again; Ingrid had left so prematurely. Her life had been cut short, far too soon. At least she left a part of herself that will always remind them of her! That was just like Ingrid, always needing to be taken care of. Now, she sort of regretted all those times she was hard on her. She would give anything now to hear her sister ask for something to eat. She would gladly give it to her, with no questions asked. She tried to hold back the tears, but they kept coming. Her mind took her back to their childhood when Ingrid would always follow her. Now she realized that little sisters are supposed to follow their big sisters around. That is what little sisters think big sisters are for. She wiped her tears and tried to fight back the rest. This was tearing her heart out. No matter how much she tried to get over her sister's death. She wasn't able to do so. She kept seeing her sister's face, hearing her voice repeatedly. She couldn't imagine anything that would have destroyed her more, not even her own death.

Just when she dried her final tear, her phone rang.

Cashmere... Hello

Simeon... Hey Cashmere, how are you?

Cashmere... Simeon, I am ok. How are you?

Simeon... I am fine. Are you sure you're okay?

Cashmere... No. I am not okay.

Simeon... What's wrong?

Cashmere... Well, my little sister recently passed away while giving birth.

Simeon... Oh, Cashmere, I am so sorry to hear that. Is there anything I can do for you?

Cashmere... No, I don't think so. I will be okay. Thanks for offering, though. Can I call you back tomorrow? I have to go.

Cashmere didn't even give him a chance to respond. She hung the phone up and cried again. Talking about her sister to Simeon was just too much for her. It was good to hear from him, but it wasn't the best time for her. She would apologize to him when she felt like she could do so. Hopefully, he would understand; if not, then he would just have to get over it. Instead, her focus was on Ingrid and Lil Ingrid. She didn't have time to worry about a man right now. She rested her face in her hands while tears flowed down her face. As many tears as she had shed, it surprised her she had any left.

She thought about her life and the things that had happened recently. Her mind went from Ingrid to taking money from Uncle Herbert. She knew that stealing from Uncle Herbert was more than wrong. In her mind, she felt she was justified. Since it was everybody else's fault, she was not using her ivy league degree. It was everybody else's fault she was still working for her uncle. It was everybody else's fault she was not far along in life. She had gotten so caught up in wanting to live the good life she had stopped trying to succeed. The years working at Uncle Herbert's shop seemed to fly by. Cashmere had lost touch with herself; she had lost touch with where she wanted to be. She wasn't living her life as she had intended. She wasn't anywhere near the path she had chosen for herself. She was lost; her soul was destroyed. She needed to find her way back in her direction. Find the Cashmere she once wanted to be instead of settling for the Cashmere that she had become. She needed to regain her focus and live life as it was supposed to be. She hadn't really thought about this in years. It would take Ingrid's death to make her realize that she had gone astray and needed to change her reality. She knew she had to stop taking money from Uncle Herbert. If she did, she wouldn't be able to afford to live. Uncle Herbert didn't pay her nearly enough to survive, much less enjoy her life. He had to know that she wasn't earning a liveable wage. Is it possible he knew that she was taking the money? If he knew, why hadn't he said anything? Was he waiting for her to confess her actions? She knew that to make things right, she had to tell him everything. Hopefully, he would not turn her into the police. She knew that it would hurt him and hurt him badly. It would shatter his trust in her for life; he always said she was his favorite niece. You can bet he wouldn't be saying that anymore. She gathered her composure. Now she was done reflecting on everything she had done wrong in her life for the past several years. She needed to relax, to unwind. She needed to just clear her mind. She went to the refrigerator and grabbed a bottle of Moscato. After getting a wine glass out of the cabinet, she sat at the table and poured the Moscato until it filled the glass. It wasn't a five ounces kind of night. She turned that glass up and finished it like it was water. She grabbed the bottle again, pouring more wine. This time she took a sip. The previous glass seemed to take the edge off. She grabbed her drink and went to the living room to listen to music. There wouldn't be any rhythm and blues tonight. She needed something that would lift her spirits. Something that would get her hyped. It depressed her; she had been mournful for several days. She needed something to take all that away, at least for tonight anyway.

The go-to music that took her to that next level was that straight gangsta rap. Whenever she listened to that, she got turnt up. She cranked the stereo volume and let the music flow through her; it didn't take long for her head to start bobbing. That gangsta music was pulling her out of her funk. She poured more Moscato, eased the glass to her mouth, and let the deliciousness from the grapes please her palette. Before long, she wasn't feeling any pain. The Moscato had taken effect. She was very relaxed by the time she made it to bed. It didn't take long for her eyes to close for the night.

Chapter 27

Tammy rolled out of bed, feeling very rested. It was great sleeping in her own bed for a change. It was a beautiful day in Virginia. She sat outside on the patio to enjoy the beautiful sun-filled morning. It really made her appreciate being back home. She enjoyed her vacation, but there was nothing like being in your own home. She had to get in touch with Cashmere to check on her. The last she heard, Ingrid was having complications with the pregnancy. She meant to reach out to Cashmere, but the cruise got in the way. She had a bad feeling about all of this. She was still reluctant to reach out to her. She wasn't exactly sure what Cashmere would have to say about Ingrid. She was hoping for the best. Unfortunately, she feared the worst. Nevertheless, she knew that it was time to contact Cashmere. She fixed herself a cup of coffee, returned to the patio, and called her.

Cashmere... Hello.

Tammy... Hey girl, how are you?

Cashmere... I have been better. How are you?

Tammy... I am glad to be back home. What's going on?

Tammy could hear Cashmere sniffling as if she were crying.

Cashmere... Well, a lot has happened since we last talked. So much has happened. I am not sure where to start.

Tammy... How about at the beginning?

Cashmere... Okay, I will try to get through this as best as possible. Ingrid went into premature labor. They tried to stop the delivery because the baby was breech, and the cord was wrapped around her neck.

Tammy... Oh my God.

Cashmere... Yeah, we found out that Ingrid had a heart condition. The doctors said that delivering the baby could prove fatal for her.

Tammy... Oh no, Cashmere.

Cashmere... They ended up having to take the baby, Ingrid fought hard for her life, but unfortunately, she passed away in the OR.

Tammy... No, Cashmere! No. Oh, hell no! She's not gone! She was too young! How are you holding up?

Cashmere... How do you think I am holding up? My little sister just died!

Tammy... I know. What a stupid question. I am so sorry, Cashmere. I'm on my way over.

Before Cashmere could respond, Tammy disconnected the call and was on her way to her car. Tammy couldn't stop the tears from running down her face. She called Char and Stephanie and asked them to meet at Cashmere's house. By the time the three of them got there, Cashmere was face down at the kitchen table with tears all over her face. Char pulled Cashmere up, and the four hugged one another until Cashmere said, "I'm all right. I'm all right." When they stopped hugging, it filled them all with tears. "I can't believe she's gone. I can't believe it!" Cashmere said before sitting down at the table again. "We're here for you, Cashmere. Your sisters are here! We will get through this together." Tammy said. They all sat down at the table, eyes filled with tears. This was a trying day for the sisterhood. "Do you need us to do anything? Do you need help with anything?" Stephanie asked. "Well, I don't know how we will pay for this funeral." "Say no more. I will cover the funeral and the hospital bills." Char said. "I can't ask you to do that, Char." "You didn't ask Cashmere, I offered. That's what sisters are for." "We are sisters forever, ladies. There is nothing that can destroy that. You ladies are my world!" Tammy said. "Cashmere, what do you have in here to eat? We may as well eat something while we are here. I'll whip something up for us real quick." Stephanie said as she was getting up to look for food. "Damn, Cashmere, there isn't enough food here to feed a starving roach. Let's go to the restaurant. We'll get something to eat there." Stephanie said. "I don't really feel like going anywhere right now." Cashmere stated. "I understand, but it might do you good to get out of here for a little. Besides, we got back in town, so we need to hang out a bit." Tammy said. "Okay, I'll go. Just for a little, though."

The girls got themselves together and rode over to Rains. By the time they got there, the place was packed with customers. They went directly back to the kitchen, where Stephanie made them plates of whatever they desired. The girls sat at a table, talking about Ingrid and all the good times they remembered having with her. It was one great memory after another. When they finished their meals, they shared several memories of Ingrid. Tears streamed down their faces. But, instead of sadness, there were tears of joy around the table. For the first time, Cashmere smiled. She had laughed; she had felt relief. She was glad her girls were there with her to make her feel better, even if it was for a brief period. She needed this more than anything right now. She knew that she didn't have to go through this alone. Her girls would be there for her. They would help her get through this. In time she would heal, and things would get easier. She would never forget Ingrid, but she would have to make good on her promise to Ingrid at some point.

Lil Ingrid would come home from the hospital soon. "Tell us about the baby. How is she doing?" Char said. "Her name is Ingrid. We call her Lil Ingrid. She is doing better. It was a scary ride at first since she was born prematurely. We didn't know if she would make it for a while. She had been in the NICU unit for several days. They finally got her weight up, and everything functions like it should be. So she should be able to come home in a few days." "We would love to meet her!" Stephanie said with a huge smile.

Chapter 28

Rico woke up the following day to a text from Crush.

Crush... Good seeing you yesterday, nephew. I'll be in touch!

There wasn't a need to reply. Knowing exactly what that meant. Crush would call to collect soon. Damn, that was not the way Rico wanted to live his life anymore. He had put that behind him and was trying to go legit. Now, he had to pay his debt to Crush. This was not a good situation for him to be in. He texts R.J. to tell him about what just happened.

Rico... Yo!

R.J.... What's up?

Rico... My uncle just hit me, saying he would be in touch soon.

R.J.... What does that mean?

Rico... It means he will ask for a favor soon.

R.J.... Damn, we need to pay him quickly.

Rico... Yeah, but we don't have it all right now.

R.J.... We could have it all by next week, though.

Rico... How do you figure that out? The rent for the club is due next week too.

R.J.... Leave it to me; I will take care of it.

Rico... Hell no! You're the reason we're in this mess.

R.J.... Oh, so now we will place blame?

Rico... Am I wrong? Damn, right, we are placing blame!

R.J. Whatever, man! Don't worry about it, I will take care of it!

Rico... How?

Rico waited for a few minutes for R.J.'s reply. There wasn't one. R.J. had stopped texting. That meant he would not tell him what he was up to. Rico had to find out. He couldn't have R.J. getting them into another situation. They were already in over their heads. Crush was family, but anybody who knew him knew that you didn't cross him. He was quick to check a fool. It didn't matter if you were blood or not. The only bright spot to this was that Rico knew he was his favorite nephew. Their only choice was to either pay him the money or do the favor when he called. He would definitely call! There was a knock at the door. Rico wasn't expecting anybody. When he peeked through the peephole, he saw a vision of loveliness standing on the other side of the door. He opened it, and Tammy was smiling ear to ear. "Hey, baby! Sorry, I stopped by, but I have missed you terribly." She stepped in and gave him the kiss of his life. "I have been missing you too, baby." He pulled her close to him and kissed her feverishly, then lifted her in the air and spun her around. "Come on in, baby. Would you like something to drink or eat?" "Well, I would like something to drink. What do you have?" "You know I have what you need, baby." "That I do!" Seeing Rico reminded her of just how much she missed him. She couldn't get close enough to him. Tammy wanted to feel him but would have to wait until later. She needed to talk to him about Ingrid. It would be hard for her to get through it without tearing up, but she had to tell him. She required his strength to help her deal with this. Her mood had changed, the smile had left, and he could see the hurt in her eyes. "Baby, are you okay?" He asked. "No, Rico, I am not. I need to talk to you about something." "What's going on, baby?" "Let's sit down for a minute." They went to the couch, and she sat beside him, taking his hand in hers. "Rico, when we were on our cruise, Cashmere got a call from Ingrid. She was at the hospital in labor." Rico waited for her to continue. Tammy took a breath and continued. "Rico, she was in premature labor. They found out the baby was in a breach, and the cord was wrapped around her little neck. Unfortunately, Ingrid found out she had a heart condition, and delivering the baby could be fatal. So, they ended up taking the baby. She just moved out of NICU, so she should come home soon." "How is Ingrid?" "Well, that's the hard part. Ingrid passed away from the delivery." Rico just sort of sat there in disbelief. Although he didn't know Ingrid that well, he knew her. He knew how close she was to the sisterhood. Tears ran down her face.

Rico put his arm around her. "Baby, how are Cashmere and Uncle Herbert? Is there anything we can do?" "I haven't spoken to Uncle Herbert, but I imagine he is just as distraught as the rest. We saw Cashmere yesterday.

She was a mess. We all were a mess!" He continued to hold her, to give her that comfort she needed. Tammy was beside herself with emotions. As much as she tried to keep it together, she couldn't. Her tears continued to flow, and Rico was there to catch everyone. As far as it concerned him, she could cry for as long as she wanted. He would just be there for her. That was what he was there for, to be there for her! She knew he would take care of her; she knew he had her back. Rico was precisely what she needed! She knew he would hold her until she fell asleep or felt better, whichever came first. She laid her head on his chest. The smell of her hair was so lovely that he couldn't help but to want to touch her. It had been two weeks since they made love. He would refrain, though, because Tammy needed comfort right now. He knew he would make love to her again, real soon. It's just that he was getting turned on by her being so close and smelling so wonderful. He kissed her on the top of her head and said, "I love you, baby!"

Chapter 29

Stephanie was happy to be back at her restaurant. She was in her office, going over her inventory. She needed to make an order for some more products before the end of the week. Rains had been doing quite well since it opened. Stephanie had quite the following now and a crowd of people almost every night. The tables were always busy. Some nights, there was a line out the door. The business was fabulous! After placing her order, she went to the dining room to greet some of her customers. Many of them she had known before she opened the restaurant. Some of them were friends of the family, and some of them she met after the restaurant opened.

While greeting one of her patrons, she noticed a face she hadn't seen in a while. It brought a smile to her face when he walked in; Detective Cruz saw her and shot a smile in her direction. She excused herself from the table and walked over to him. "Aren't you a sight for sore eyes?" He said. "Well, hello there, detective. How are you doing these days?" "I'm fine; please feel free to call me Caleb." "Caleb, okay, Caleb. Please come on in and have a seat. What can I do for you today?" "Well, I was hoping I would get an answer about that dinner." "You are quite the persistent one, aren't you?" "I can be when I really want something or someone!" "Oh, is that right? So, you really want me?" She couldn't help but smile after saying that. She was curious as to what his answer would be. "Of course, I would love to get to know you better! I think you could be one of the special ones." That definitely put a smile on her face. She knew he was playing it safe, trying not to be rude or too forward, but he did get his point across. "One of the special ones. I don't think I have ever heard that one before." "Well, I am an original kind of guy. Wait until you really get to know me. You won't be able to get enough of me." "You're quite sure of yourself, aren't you?" "Well, there's nothing wrong with a little confidence. I tell you, why don't you get to know me and see for yourself." Caleb gave her a very inviting smile. He definitely had an air of confidence about him. Stephanie kind of liked that. She thought dinner with him would be interesting. "Okay, Caleb, I will have dinner with you. When should we do this?" "How about tomorrow night? I'll pick you up around seven." "Okay, that sounds good. I will be ready." Caleb smiled, feeling like he had accomplished something. He gave her a hug, then he turned and left. Stephanie watched him until he exited Rains. She hoped she had done the right thing by agreeing to have dinner with him. He seemed like a nice enough guy. She knew for sure that she would be safe around him. He had piqued into her interests. She was curious to see how the night would go. It would be an exciting evening if it went like their encounter a few minutes ago. A smile eased on her face; it had been some time since she had been on a date. She had been so consumed with getting her restaurant off the ground that she hadn't found the time for a social life. She was rusty, out of practice. Hopefully, Caleb wouldn't notice. Hopefully, things would fall right into place for her. She was starting to get a little excited. She couldn't take her mind off of her date tomorrow night.

Although she needed to return to work, she stopped thinking about the date and started thinking about the restaurant again. She was going to add a new dish to the menu, and she needed to ensure that she had all the ingredients to prepare the dish for the crew to taste. The dish was a mouthwatering baked Alaskan cod entree she had encountered on her vacation. Stephanie simply fell in love with the dish. She had to try and replicate it; of course, she would put her own spin on her plate. It had to be distinct to her style of cooking. If it wasn't, it just wouldn't be Stephanie. Her customers had come to expect nothing short of greatness regarding her dishes. They knew that she took great pride in preparing them to perfection. She wanted her customers to have a mouthwatering experience each time they dined at Rains. She knew that they had a choice; she was fortunate that they chose to spend their time and money at her restaurant. People were starting to filter in. The tables were beginning to fill up. There were already several people at the bar enjoying cocktails. By the time Stephanie looked up, she had been at the restaurant for quite some time. She hadn't noticed the hours going by. She had been enjoying being back in her restaurant. Upon entering the kitchen, she smelled the flavors emanating from the pots on the stoves. Her nose was pleasantly pleased with flavorful goodness. As she looked around the kitchen, she couldn't help but smile. She had accomplished one of her goals. She had achieved her dream. Life was good for her right now, and she knew it.

Chapter 30

By the time Char had opened her eyes, the evening had settled in. She had slept for quite some time. She sent a text to Cashmere to check on her.

Char... Hey Cashmere, how are you?

Cashmere... I am doing okay. How are you?

Char... Just woke up. Worrying about you.

Cashmere... I appreciate it, but I will be okay. Just need to get things taken care of for Ingrid.

Char... I know. I understand. You know we are here for you if you need us.

Cashmere... Thank you very much.

Char... You're welcome. Call me if you need anything, and I mean anything.

She knew she would have to check on Cashmere more often. She would need her girls more than ever. Cashmere always tried to play it cool, like she always had it together. Char knew her well. She knew that Cashmere wouldn't ask for help. She would try to do everything independently, just like when she wouldn't accept the cruise ticket. She had to pay for it on her own.

She went by Cashmere's just to see how she was really doing. By the time she arrived, she couldn't tell if Cashmere was even home. She walked up to the door, knocked, and waited for a few seconds. There weren't any sounds. She knocked again! "Cashmere... are you home?" Nothing! Not one sound. Luckily, Char knew where the spare key lived. She grabbed it, opened the door, and walked in. "Cashmere, it's me, Char! Are you home?" She paused for a response. Again there was nothing. She closed the door and walked through the house, looking for Cashmere. When she got to the upstairs bedroom, she heard the shower running. A sigh of relief escaped as she exhaled. She had the most horrible feeling that something had happened to Cashmere. It was good to know that she was just taking a shower.

She scribed a note on a piece of paper and left it on her pillow. "I'm downstairs. Char."

She went straight to the kitchen, opened the fridge, and pulled out a bottle of Moscato. She poured a glass, gulped it down, then poured another. She was still trying to ease her mind about thinking the worst about Cashmere. "I hope you will pour me a glass since you are drinking my wine without me," Cashmere said as she walked into the kitchen. "Most certainly. How are you feeling?" Char replied. Cashmere grabbed a glass out of the cabinet while Char poured another, then one for her. "Things are rough for me right now. I have been trying to take care of things for Ingrid. It's just so hard to do this right now. There's so much going through my mind right now." "Do you want to talk about it?" "I really don't know where to start. I don't even know what to say. I wish I didn't have to go through any of this. I wish Ingrid was still here. I wish I could just call her and tell her I love her so much! And then there is little Ingrid. What am I supposed to do with her? Can I really raise, excuse me, help raise a child with a man I couldn't care less about? Of all the men in the world, why did she have to pick one I dated? Who am I kidding? I can't even get my life on track." She couldn't hold back the tears any longer. They flowed out of her like heavy rain hitting the pavement. "Why did she have to do this? Why? Why did she have to die? I can't do this. I can't do any of this! I keep wishing that one day, I will wake up, and this will all be some horrible dream. Ingrid will be okay; she'll be right here, eating all my damn food." Char just listened. She didn't speak. She didn't want to interrupt her. She knew she needed to get all of this out of her system. She needed to purge and deal with the loss of her sister. Cashmere's tears kept coming. They wouldn't stop. No matter how many she wiped from her face, they continued to fall. "The worst part about this damn thing is that little Ingrid will never know what a wonderful person her mother was. She will never get to talk to her. She will never get to know her. Never!!!!!" Char just kept listening, letting Cashmere talk. "Now, I must deal with the aftermath of all of this. I have to help raise my niece with that no-good ass, Damian. I hated him so much in school. I still can't stand him. No matter what he says, something tells me he knew Ingrid and I were sisters." "Cashmere, what happened with him anyway? I don't think I ever heard the story." Cashmere paused, wiping the tears from her eyes. "Well, he started out as a nice guy. We did our homework together, and he walked me home from school. We went out a few times, and I thought we were progressing nicely. Then, we went to one of his friends' houses to hang out. They were drinking, and he asked me to have some too. I reluctantly did so. Suddenly, I felt funny, like something was wrong. I told him I needed to go home. He said, "Don't worry about it. Everything will be okay." He kissed and touched me, then his friend sat down beside me and touched me. Damian just let him do it. That's when I realized they had drugged me and tried to have sex with me." "What happened after that?" "I pushed Damian away, got up, and ran out of the house. I cried home because I thought he was a nice guy." "What happened when you saw him again?" "I said nothing else to him. Every time I saw him, I would just look away." "Have you two ever talked about it?" "No, of course not. I put it all behind me until I saw him enter the hospital room." "So, you haven't had closure yet. You have to talk to him about it at some point. How will you help raise little Ingrid if you don't resolve this between you?" "Honestly, I don't know what to say to him. I'm not sure I can talk to him without getting infuriated. I would probably want to do serious harm to him." Char knew that Cashmere wasn't playing. She had a temper and would surely act on it. It may have been what Damian had tried that gave her the thick skin she had. To talk to him about this would definitely be monumental for her. She had vowed she would let no one else take advantage of her again, especially him. Yet, she hadn't faced him.

She hadn't given him a piece of her mind yet. Char was right; she needed to talk to him about it. She needed to tell him she wasn't okay with any of it. That would be the only way they could move forward with what they needed to do. It was in the best interests of little Ingrid. And that was truly all that mattered.

Chapter 31

Char had been back in town for a week and was due to fly out again. This time she was headed to Honolulu, where she would do runway modeling at the most prominent fashion show of the year. That was something she truly loved to do. It was something about walking down that runway in the most glamorous clothing, designed by the most influential who's who of fashion, under the same roof simultaneously. It had attracted her to modeling; fame and fortune didn't hurt either. This would be the perfect situation for her to pitch her clothing line. There would be many of the hottest designers there. She knew she was well respected in the modeling game, so it wouldn't be a problem for any of them to look at her line. She was determined to bring "From My Mother's Closet" to fruition. This would transition her from modeling to designing. She felt it was time to venture on to the next endeavor.

The morning arrived for her to fly out. She woke up feeling anything but rested. She had spent most of the night tossing and turning. All she could think about was that Ingrid was gone. Ingrid had always been around. When she was little, she tried to follow them everywhere they went. She knew that Cashmere needed more attention from everybody. She wanted to be there for Cashmere, but her schedule was far too demanding.

Her car arrived a few minutes early. It was 8am when she walked out the door. When she got in the limo, she grabbed an apple juice to sip on while she text Cashmere.

Char... Hey girl, you up yet?

Cashmere... Yeah, been up for a while now. Why?

Char... Headed to Honolulu for a few days. Thought I would check on you before I left.

Cashmere... I am well, thanks. You don't really have to check on me. I will be just fine.

Char... I know you are. I wanted to hear you say it.

Cashmere... Why is that?

Char... Just to make sure you knew you would bounce back from this. I know it's hard to deal with, but I am sure. Eventually, it will be easier to deal with as time passes.

Cashmere... I am sure you're right. I pray that it gets easier soon.

Char... Have you decided when the funeral will be?

Cashmere... It will be this Saturday at 11am. Will you be back by then?

Char... I get back Friday night at midnight, so I will be back by then.

Cashmere... Great, I hope you can make it.

Char... You know I wouldn't miss that. I will be there for sure.

Cashmere... That's good. You know I will need my girls there to help me through this.

Char... That is a given. We'll be there for you, that's for sure!

Cashmere... I know you will be there for me. I'm sorry, Char, but I can't talk anymore.

Char... Okay, I'll check on you later.

Char waited for a reply, one she knew she wouldn't receive any time soon. She knew that Cashmere was more than likely crying her eyes out. No matter how much they talked about it. No matter how much they tried to get over it, this would be the hardest thing for any of them to get over, especially Cashmere. "What time does my plane leave," Char asked the driver. "Ma'am, your plane leaves in 90 minutes." "Great, then we have time to stop by Cashmere's place before we go." "Are you sure, ma'am? It is a 45-minute drive to the airport, and you still have to get to your gate." "Yes, I am certain. Please take me to Cashmere's before we go to the airport." The driver knew that they would have a hard time making it to the airport if they stopped by Cashmere's on the way. But, knowing that the customer was always right, he did as he was asked.

When they arrived at Cashmere's house, Char walked up to the door. The door was opened, and she could hear music playing. She called for Cashmere, but there wasn't an answer. She called again. Still no answer. Char opened the screen door and walked in. She was cautious because she didn't know what to expect. She walked around the place, calling for Cashmere. There wasn't an answer. Then she heard the front door close. She went towards the door and saw Cashmere standing in the living room. "Char, what in the hell are you doing here? I thought you were on your way to Hawaii." "I was. I mean, I am. I stopped by to see you before I left." "Why Char? I told you I was fine. You didn't need to stop by here." "I know, but I was worried about you. I didn't want to leave town until I knew you were okay." "Char, to be honest with you, I will never be okay again. My sister just died. It will take everything I have to continue on. I have to deal with this on my own. I appreciate you stopping by going to the airport. Call me when you land." Cashmere walked over to the door and opened it for Char to walk through. "Are you sure?" "Yes, I am sure, Char. Go to Hawaii." I'll see you when you get back. Char looked at Cashmere, walked out the door, and went to the limo. The whole time she walked to the car, she had that eerie feeling that Cashmere wasn't being truthful. It scared her that Cashmere would do something crazy. When she got back in the car, she text Tammy.

Char... Tammy, I am going out of town for a few days. I left Cashmere's place. I have a funny feeling about her. Could you please check on her over the next couple of days?

Tammy... Why do you feel that way? What happened? What did she say?

Char... She said she was okay and didn't need me checking on her. I don't feel right about the whole thing. I would feel better if I knew you were checking up on her.

Tammy... Okay, I will check on her tonight before I go to The Crib.

Char... Why don't you see if she wants to go with you?

Tammy... That's a good idea. I'll ask her soon. Have a safe trip, Char.

Char... Great, let me know if anything seems crazy about her. Thanks, I will.

Tammy... This is Cashmere we're talking about, right? Everything is crazy about her.

Char... True. Well, you know what I mean.

Tammy... I get you, though; I will let you know if anything strange happens.

Char... Great, thanks.

Tammy... Of course.

Chapter 32

Tammy decided to drop by Cashmere's place instead of calling or texting her. She knew that Cashmere would have an attitude about it but didn't give a damn about it. She was determined to make sure that Cashmere wouldn't do anything crazy. So, she stopped by the store and picked up a couple of bottles of Moscato. When she arrived at Cashmere's place, the door was opened, and she heard music playing in the distance. "Cashmere," she said as she rang the doorbell. "Really? What is with you and Char? Why do y'all keep popping up at my place? Don't you know it is polite to call before you come?"

"Yeah, we know it is more polite to call first, but we also know that you will tell us that you are fine, even though you may not be. So, I need to see for myself. But, sorry, I can't take your word for it. I need to put my eyes on you!" "Whatever," Cashmere said as she opened the door. "Besides, I came bearing gifts." "I see; you know where the wine glasses are." Cashmere made her way to the living room, plopped down on the couch, and waited for Tammy to return with the wine. "Hello, hospitable much. This is your place, you know." Cashmere just sort of laughed. "It's not like you're a guest here. I don't have to cater to you."

"Yeah, you must be doing okay. Same ole Cashmere, I see." "I told you both, I am fine. It's just something I have to deal with." No Cashmere. We all have to deal with it. Ingrid may have been your biological sister, but she was like a sister to all of us. She means something to us too." "I know, and thank you for that. That means a lot to me. I'm trying to get past this, but it is so hard. Sometimes, I think I hear her voice. When I look at little Ingrid, I see so much of Ingrid in her." "Speaking of little Ingrid, where is she?" "She's upstairs sleeping." "May I go up and take a peek at her?" "Of course, please try and be quiet, though. I just put her down. I need her to sleep for a while." "Great, I'll be right back."

Tammy went up to see little Ingrid, leaving Cashmere downstairs. She eased in as quietly as possible when she got to the room. Little Ingrid stirred a little bit as Tammy gazed at her. She was beautiful. Simply gorgeous. She looked just like Ingrid. Tammy just couldn't believe that

Ingrid was gone. A tear started to run down her face, and she felt a deep pain in her chest. Her heart was hurting for Cashmere and Little Ingrid. This was too much for anybody to have to deal with. The more she thought about it, the more the tears flowed. "It's okay, Tammy. Everything will be alright. It has to be right," Cashmere said as she put her arm around Tammy. "Yeah, it has to be. You don't have to do this alone. We will be right here to help you through it all." "I know. I know. Come on, let's go back downstairs before she wakes up."

When they returned to the living room, Cashmere's phone was ringing.

Cashmere... Hello!

Stephanie... Hey Cashmere, how are you?

Cashmere... What is with everybody?

Stephanie... What do you mean?

Cashmere... You, Tammy, and Char. Why are all of you calling and stopping by to check on me?

Stephanie... Well, of course, I will call and make sure you are okay. That's what friends do. Stopping by. Who stopped by?

Cashmere... Char, and Tammy. Hell, Tammy is here now.

Stephanie... Tammy is there? What are y'all doing?

Cashmere... She stopped by to check on me. We're having some Moscato.

Stephanie... Moscato? I could use some of that right about now.

Cashmere... Well, come on by. Everybody else already has.

Stephanie... I am on my way.

Cashmere... Why am I not surprised?

Stephanie... Girl, stop acting like you don't want any company.

Cashmere... Whatever, I'll see you when you get here.

Stephanie... Alright, see you soon.

Cashmere hung up the phone. "Stephanie is on the way too." "Nice, I guess we are having a little get-together tonight. Maybe we should check out The Crib too." "I don't think so. I'm not sure I want to be around many people right now." "That might be what you need to take your mind off everything for a little while." "Easier said than done. I'm not really feeling like going out." "That's why you should go out. You need to have a little fun. Besides, you know Ingrid wouldn't want you to not enjoy yourself." "Don't you do that! Don't you say what Ingrid would or wouldn't want? Not now, not yet!" Cashmere lost it; her tears flooded her face. She couldn't control herself. Tammy tried to console her as much as possible, but Cashmere was far too gone to reel her back in. Then Tammy decided to let her cry it all out of her system. She needed to get it all out anyway. Cashmere had been trying her best to stay strong. But, sometimes, situations occur that you can't be firm about. This was definitely one of them.

The doorbell rang. "Coming," Tammy said. "Hey Tammy, how is Cashmere," Stephanie asked as she entered Cashmere's place. "She just lost it. I may have said the wrong thing. I may have pushed her too hard." "What did you say?" "Well, I suggested that we all go out tonight." "That isn't bad. Why would she lose it over that?" "Well, I said a little more than that." "What else did you say?" "I said that Ingrid would want you to enjoy yourself." "Oh damn, that'll do it. She wasn't ready for that one. It is too soon. She hasn't even buried her sister yet." "I know; I didn't say it to upset her. I honestly thought it would motivate her. Obviously, I was wrong." "So, what now?" "Well, I think we let her get it all out of her system and change the damn subject." "Okay, let's go in and see how she is doing."

Tammy and Stephanie went into the living room, where Cashmere was still crying. "Hey, Cashmere," Stephanie said as she sat on the couch. Cashmere was crying so much that she couldn't even utter the word hello. Stephanie just put her arms around her and said, "It is going to be okay. You cry those tears out. We'll be here for you as long as you need us!" Tammy poured another round of Moscato. Stephanie looked up and saw a picture of Ingrid and couldn't help but start to tear up. Tammy saw Stephanie tearing up, and they were all sitting there crying. Three sisters shedding tears together. All that was missing was Char.

Chapter 33

When Stephanie got home, she continued to think about Cashmere and what had just transpired. She had never seen Cashmere appear so fragile, so broken. It was a Cashmere that she hadn't experienced before. She was accustomed to seeing a fearless individual. Someone more vital than the strongest person. It made her seem, well, almost human. She saw her in a different light now. She felt her pain. She understood her struggles and the way her heart hurt. Somehow this seemed to bring her closer to Cashmere. She knew she had to make sure that Cashmere made it through this as best as she could. She needed Cashmere to get back to normal if that was possible. Losing Ingrid would change them, especially with the birth of Little Ingrid. She would be a constant reminder of their loss and their gain. This was the reality that their lives had been dealt with. They had to adapt and make their peace with it all. Cashmere would have to make the most significant adaptation. She would be the one that would have to be the strongest. Stephanie knew that the road would be hard for her. She also knew that the sisterhood would all be there to help Cashmere get through this. They would ensure she got the love she needed to overcome this unfortunate travesty.

Since they didn't go to The Crib, Stephanie was a little hungry and whipped up something light to munch on. She concocted a nice little salad and poured a nice glass of Moscato to wash it down with. Just as she was taking a forkful, her phone buzzed. She looked down at the screen, and Caleb was calling.

Stephanie... Hello!

Caleb... Hello, Stephanie. How are you?

Stephanie... Hey Caleb, I am well, thanks. How are you doing?

Caleb... That is good to know. I am great, thanks. How was your trip with your girls?

Stephanie... It was lovely. It was also somewhat saddening.

Caleb... Saddening? What do you mean by that?

Stephanie... Well, to be honest. It is a long story, and I am not sure I want to go into it now.

Caleb... Oh, okay, I understand.

Stephanie... Please don't take it the wrong way. It is very involved, and it makes me emotional.

Caleb... I get it. I understand, and no worries. I didn't take it the wrong way.

Stephanie... Great, I am glad you understand.

Caleb... Subject change. Do you still want to go out tonight, or do you need some time to yourself?

Stephanie... Yes. I am looking forward to it.

Caleb... Great. I am looking forward to it too.

Stephanie... That is good to know.

Caleb... Great! I'll pick you up tonight at about 7:30.

Stephanie... 7:30 would be fine. Let's meet up if you want.

Caleb... A true gentleman, will always pick you up.

Stephanie... Nice reply.

Caleb... So, I will see you at 7:30.

Stephanie... Yes, you will. I look forward to it.

Caleb... Great, see you then!

Stephanie... Okay, bye.

Stephanie ended the call. She was a little nervous about accepting the date, but she was interested in seeing how the date would go. It had piqued her interest.

When Caleb ended the call, he couldn't help but smile. He had gotten her to agree to have dinner with him. His confidence had proven to be fruitful. Now, all he had to do was charm her into wanting to have another date. His game plan was set. He knew he had to step his game up to get her interest. So far, so good for him. Now to take care of the reservations for tonight. Since she is a restaurant owner, he would have to take her somewhere that would blow her mind. He only had a few hours to do his research and come up with the perfect place. His outfit had to be on point. He wanted to impress her the whole night, and it would all start with his attire.

Chapter 34

Rico woke up to birds chirping and a gentle breeze flowing through his opened bedroom window. It was nice to see Tammy last night. He would hopefully make plans to see her later tonight. He missed her more than words could convey. It felt good to hold her in his arms. He knew she was going through something horrible. But, he also knew that he would do anything he had to do to help her get through this.

Something else troubling him was that she might discover what went down at the club with Crush. This was a secret he would try to take to his grave, but everybody knows that what's done in the dark always comes to light. It might not be today, tomorrow, or even next year, but it will soon rear its ugly head. It always does! And if she found out, it would destroy his relationship with her. There wouldn't be a way that their relationship could survive it. But, to tell you the truth, he couldn't blame her either. If the shoe was on the other foot, he would probably feel the same way, no matter how much he loved her.

Rico showered and prepared a small breakfast before he got on the road. He needed to stop by the cafe for a few hours before meeting up with R.J. at The Crib. When he got to the cafe, customers settled in for their breakfast. The cafe had always been a great place to eat, but they were most known for their incredible breakfast. That was always the busiest shift, then lunch seemed to run a close second. By dinner time, the customers would thin out considerably, except on the weekends. Rico grabbed a tray and took orders from the customers. Although he didn't need to work there, he still liked to help. He got along well with the workers and had grown fond of some locals that frequented the establishment.

After a few hours at the cafe, Rico rode to Colonial Heights. First, he needed to stop by Southpark Mall. There was something there that he thought Tammy would just adore. When he got there, he walked around some shops; Rico had time to kill before he needed to pick up Tammy's surprise. Next, he stopped in a few clothing stores; he wanted to pick up a couple pairs of jeans and some shirts. When he finished, he went to the jewelry store to acquire Tammy's surprise. The lady behind the counter smiled at him when he walked in. She had been the one that had helped him pick out the perfect surprise for her.

"Hello, is it ready?" "Yes, it is ready. I'll get it for you." While Rico waited for the salesperson to return, he walked around the store, looking at watches. He saw several he liked. When she returned, she handed him the surprise. "This is amazing," he stated. "It is beautiful. I am sure she will like it." "I hope so. This is a special gift for a special person." "Any woman would love to have a gift like this." Rico was thrilled with his choice. He couldn't help but smile as he thought about the look on her face when he gave it to her. She will be so happy! Rico walked away from the store feeling great about his purchase. He couldn't help but think about that first day he met her at the cafe. He noticed her from the time she walked in the door. Of all the people that walked in that cafe, she was the only one that made him look twice. She had come into his life and changed him. Made him care about something more than just himself. She was the one that called out to his heart. He thought back and wondered how he had ever lived without her. Life now seemed so complete for him with her in it. It was time for him to take their relationship to the next level. They've been doing this for a minute now. He knew she was the one for him. Yep, it was time to put a ring on it.

Now all he had to do was set up the perfect night to propose. But, he had to find something that would blow her mind. Something they both would remember for the rest of their lives. He had the perfect plan. He knew just how he would do it. Now, to put it all together.

Chapter 35

The dreaded day had finally arrived. It was the funeral day! It would be the most challenging day of Cashmere's life. Today, she would lay her little sister to rest.

When she arrived at the church, people were already starting to gather. She sat at the front, right in front of the casket. Looking at her sister, she couldn't help but think she looked just as beautiful as ever. Ingrid had always been an attractive girl. The funeral home did a fantastic job. She tried to fight back the tears, but the more she looked at Ingrid, the more tears befell her face. "Hey baby, have you been here long," Uncle Herbert asked. "No, Uncle Herbert, I arrived just a few minutes ago." "Come on, let's take Lil Ingrid to meet her mother," Uncle Herbert stated. Cashmere hesitated for a few seconds before joining her uncle and Lil Ingrid at the casket. "Lil Ingrid, this is your mother. You may never speak to her, but always know she will be with you. She will always be a part of you," Uncle Herbert said emotionally. Cashmere touched Ingrid's hand and said, "Don't worry, sis, I've got here for you. I will make sure she grows up right!" "Yeah, we both will!" A voice from behind them said. They both turned to see Damian standing there. Cashmere returned to her seat, and Damian stepped up to the casket.

Uncle Herbert gave him Lil Ingrid and stepped away to provide them with time with Ingrid alone. "Ingrid. Oh, Ingrid, I am so sorry that you aren't able to see how beautiful our daughter is. She is amazing. I can't thank you enough for this blessing. I only wish you were alive to see her for yourself. She has your eyes! Oh, and she has your cute little nose too." Damian held Lil Ingrid in one arm and held Ingrid's hand with the other. "Baby, I never thought it would come to this. I thought we would have forever; I thought we would be happy together. I wanted forever with you. I miss you, baby. I love you so much!" Cashmere saw a side of Damian that she had never seen before as his face filled with tears. She heard true love in his voice and saw adoration on his face. She could tell that he was genuinely hurting. At first, she doubted his intentions for Ingrid, but now she knew he was genuinely in love with her. She walked up next to him, touched his arm, and guided him back to the pew where she and Uncle Herbert were sitting.

There was so much she wanted to say to him, so many questions she wanted to ask but didn't. She would wait until later to say what was on her mind. Then, finally, the congregation filled up the church. The pastor walked up to the pulpit. It was time to start the service; the church fell silent and awaited the pastor's opening words. Char, Tammy, and Stephanie were all there. They had found seats next to Cashmere; they wouldn't have it any other way. Tammy sat next to Cashmere. She held her hand to give her the strength she needed to make it through this.

By the time the pastor finished the sermon, there wasn't a dry eye in the church. The pallbearers carried the body out to the white hearse, placed her in it, and the procession began. When they arrived at the gravesite, many people were still crying. They gathered around as the pastor said a few words, then it was time for everyone to say their final goodbyes to Ingrid. Cashmere waited for everyone to say their goodbyes before she went up. Finally, Uncle Herbert and Damian went up before her. Damian broke down again, and Uncle Herbert walked away with him. Finally, Cashmere went up to tell her goodbyes to her dear sister.

"Ingrid, where do I start? You were always my little sister. I want to hang out with my girls. Had I known our time was limited, I would have embraced every opportunity. I am sorry I didn't treat you like I should have. It's not that I didn't love you. It's not that I didn't want you around. It's just that I didn't know how to be a better big sister to you. And now you're gone. I'll never get the chance to make it up to you. Never get the chance to tell you how much you really meant. But, I promise you that I will ensure that Lil Ingrid knows everything about you. I will make sure she grows up to be respectful and mannerable. I will make sure she grows up just like you, little sister. I love you so much. Until I see you again, I know you'll be watching! Goodbye, sis!"

They lowered the coffin, and Cashmere took that moment to walk away. She couldn't bear seeing them lower the coffin. That was just too much to handle. Her tears flowed down her face on her way back to the limo. When she got in the limo, her girls were waiting for her. She sat down beside Char. There was an awkward silence for what seemed like a lifetime before someone uttered a word. "Cashmere, we love you so much! We are here for you, girl," Stephanie said. "I know you guys are. Thank you all for being there for me. I really need you now. I don't know what I will do." "You will make it through this. You'll see, it will be hard, but we'll get through it together," Char said.

Silence once again befell the limo. The girls realized they had just left a part of themselves at that grave site. A portion of themselves that they would never forget. A piece that meant the world to all of them. Ingrid had journeyed on to a better place. She would forever be in their hearts! Forever!!!!!

Chapter 36

Caleb pulled up to Stephanie's place, nerves on edge. His mind was racing a mile a minute. He needed this date to go perfectly because she didn't know it, but Stephanie had his nose wide open. When he saw her, he couldn't stop thinking about her. She enticed him. He wanted to know more about her. So tonight, he would lay the foundation to do just that.

He walked up to the door and rang the bell. It was a matter of seconds before he heard the click of high heels heading towards the door. It seemed like she took an eternity to open the door. He was delighted with what he saw when the door opened. She was as stunning as he expected. Her hair laid on her shoulders, just right. Her smile was sexy with a hint of confidence. It said, "Are you ready for me?" to him. She invited him in. As he passed her, he would get a whiff of her perfume. A scent that made him even more impressed with her. She looked great, and also, she knew it. "I need to grab my purse, and I will be ready." "Great, I'll wait right here." He watched her walk down the hallway, heels clicking against the tiled floor. He couldn't take his eyes off her. She knew she held his gaze as she walked away. When she returned, he opened the door for her and enjoyed the smell of her perfume as she walked by him. He opened her car door and watched her ease into his Corvette. "So, where are we going, Caleb?" "You'll see. I hope that you will love it too!" He pulled off and headed to one of the finest restaurants in downtown Richmond. Stephanie just sat back and enjoyed the ride. They chit-chatted a little in between the awkward silences. They both were a little nervous. Caleb wasn't as confident as he was the last time they talked. Could it have been that he wasn't expecting her to be as stunning as she was? She might have thrown him off his game for a minute but knew he would bounce back and dazzle her with his smooth style and exciting conversation. When they pulled up to the restaurant, he had rebuilt his confidence. He was feeling like his old self again. He parked the car, got out, and opened the door for her. Extending his hand, she softly placed her hand in his. He watched her leave the car because he couldn't take his eyes off her. They walked in and were immediately seated. He winked at the waitress, and she knew exactly what to do. She brought out a bottle of champagne for them to enjoy. After pouring the champagne, the waiter placed a long-stemmed rose on the table for Stephanie. "For the lovely lady, compliments of Mr. Cruz," the waitress remarked with a smile. "Caleb, you didn't have to do this. I'm glad you did, though." "I want tonight to be special. A night we won't soon forget." They raised their glasses and toasted to what they hoped would be a great evening. Stephanie sipped the champagne as the waiter sat their menus on the table. "I'll give you two a few moments to peruse the menu. Should you have questions, I'll return in a few minutes to answer them," the waitress said. Stephanie was the first one to pick up the menu. She perused the dishes, looking to see how they compared to her menu. Once she finished, she decided that her menu was very nice. Still, it wasn't as lovely as the restaurant Caleb had chosen tonight. Her choice for the night would be the peppercorn-crusted filet mignon with a white wine sauce. At the same time, he decided on the beef bourguignon with parmesan risotto. When the waitress returned, they placed their order and refilled their champagne glasses.

"So, are you having a good time so far?" "Actually, Caleb, I am having a good time. I will be honest, though. The night started off a little scary. It seemed a little awkward in the car." "I agree. In all honesty, I was a little nervous at first. My nervousness has dissipated now, though. I am looking forward to a great evening with you." "Okay, since you admit that you were nervous. I will do the same; I was nervous myself. It has been quite some time since I have been on a date. I've had so much going on in my life that I have had little time for a social life." "I can understand that. If it wasn't for those letters you were receiving from Matthius, we wouldn't have met." True, don't remind me of that creep. He made my life miserable. I can't believe he tried to kill me. It's good that you were on the case; no telling what would have happened." "Well, one thing is for certain. As long as I am around, nothing or no one will ever get close enough to harm you again. You have my word on that young lady!" A smile eased upon her face. Caleb had scored points with that one. What's more, is that his words seemed genuine. He had this look in his eyes that held her gaze and her attention.

The waitress returned with their meals. She placed the meals in front of them. Stephanie looked at her dinner and knew she had ordered the proper meal. She couldn't wait to taste a forkful of that rich, tasty deliciousness. Caleb enjoyed the way his meal looked, but he wasn't a foodie like she was. However, he knew this restaurant had some of the most fantastic food on the East coast. It would be impressive, to say the least.

They were both more than satisfied when they finished their meals. The waitress returned with a dessert menu. "Can I offer you one of our exquisite desserts to end the night with?" "Would you like dessert, Stephanie?" "Why don't we share one?" "That sounds good." He looked at the waitress and said, "What do you recommend for a first date dessert?" "I would suggest the panna cotta or the tiramisu. They are both perfect for a first date couple to share." "Which would you choose, Stephanie?" "I would choose the panna cotta. That would be tasty." "The panna cotta it is then." "Great, I will get that for you right away." "Thank you so much," Caleb said. "I must say this is an amazing place. This was a great choice." "I was hoping you were going to like it. I had heard a lot about this place. Up to now, I had never been before. I am glad we had our first date here."

The waitress returned with their panna cotta and placed it in the middle of the table, along with two forks for them to enjoy. "Enjoy," she said before she left the table. Stephanie picked up Caleb's knife and fork, cut a small piece of the panna cotta, and placed it in front of his mouth. He opened his mouth, and she slid the fork into his mouth. The panna cotta tasted better than any dessert he had ever eaten before. He picked up Stephanie's fork, cut a small piece of the panna cotta, and placed it in front of her mouth. He fed her the panna cotta; she savored the flavor before she swallowed it. She wanted to experience the taste of every ingredient. The panna cotta melted in her mouth. It was filled with mouth-watering scrumptiousness. They fed each other until they enjoyed the rest of the dessert.

They had filled their conversation with laughter when they arrived at her place. He walked her to the door. She placed the key in the door, opened it, turned to him, and said, "Caleb, I had a great time tonight. Thank you again for a wonderful evening." He took her hand and kissed it softly. "It was my pleasure, Stephanie. I hope we can do it again, real soon." "So do I." She walked into the house, shutting the door as he walked away. She lay against the back of the door, smiling, thinking it was a great night. Little did he know, she was ready to see him again. Hopefully, he will call soon!

Chapter 37

The following day Char woke up later than she had expected. Her alarm clock had gone off, but she had slept right through it. She was exhausted from her flight back, then going to Ingrid's funeral. She really hadn't rested. She would take today to rest up and relax. She didn't plan to do anything today but just chill. Hopefully, it will stay that way too. She poured herself a tall glass of water, sat on the couch, turned the television on, and just chilled. Her thoughts took her in many directions. One thought that kept popping up was her clothing line. She was preparing to start the line in a few months. They had completed the legwork. All that was left was to present it to the world. She would promote it at every event she attended going forward. Soon From My Mother's Closet would be in every store, every closet in America. That was her goal anyway.

Char opened the French doors that led to her deck. It was a gorgeous day. The sun was shining, and a gentle breeze brushed against her skin. Char prepared herself some breakfast and would have it out on the deck. She mixed up a mimosa to enjoy with her breakfast. The morning seemed to go well, going just as planned. She wanted an excellent breakfast, to be outside, listen to the birds' chirp, and feel a nice breeze. After Char finished washing her dishes, she sat back on the couch. Just when she found a movie to watch, her phone rang.

Char... Hello!

Stephanie... Hey girl, how are you doing?

Char... I am well. How are you, Stephanie?

Stephanie... I am good girl. I am terrific.

Char... Real good, huh? What's up with that?

Stephanie... Well, since you asked. I went out with Caleb last night.

Char... I take it the date went well?

Stephanie... It started out a little awkward, but as the night went on, it turned out great!

Char... That sounds nice. Why was it awkward at first?

Stephanie... Well, when we were going to dinner, it was quiet in the car. You know that awkward silence.

Char... Oh, okay, was he nervous? Were you nervous?

Stephanie... Yeah, we both were a little nervous. Once we got that out of the way, it was great.

Char... Very nice. Well, what is he like?

Stephanie... Char, he is fantastic. He knows how to have a conversation. He seems to be romantic. He went out of his way to impress me.

Char... Sounds like you will see him again.

Stephanie... Yeah, I am. As soon as he calls me again.

Char... You know you don't have to wait for him to call. You can contact him too.

Stephanie... Yeah, I know. I think it is more appropriate for the man to call. I don't want to seem eager or desperate.

Char... Stephanie, you won't seem eager or desperate. Instead, you will seem like you had a good time and look forward to seeing him again. I think that is the most authentic way to be. No games, just straight-up realness!

Stephanie... Damn, Char, where is all this coming from? You know that's how we do things.

Char... I think if you are lucky enough to have someone interested in you, you don't need to procrastinate or play games.

Stephanie... Oh, I see now.

Char... What do you mean by that?

Stephanie... What I mean is, your work has you so busy that you don't find the time to find someone special for you.

Char... You could be right. Anyway, don't play games. If you want to see him again. Call him. There is nothing wrong with you asking him out.

Stephanie... I hear you, Char. Maybe I will do just that. All right, girl, I'm about to jump in the shower and start my day.

Char... All right, girl. I'll talk to you later.

Char hung up the phone, thinking about what Stephanie had just said. She was correct; her career kept her so busy that she didn't have a chance to find her special someone. All her girls were finding love, but she was still waiting for her special one. She was wondering if he was indeed out there. It had been quite some time since she had a serious relationship with a man. A few expressed interest, but they didn't amount to anything. They had their own agendas or were trying to run game. She didn't have time for someone that wasn't trying to be honest with her. She knew she brought a lot to the table; she didn't expect a man to bring as much as she did, but she expected him to bring something and not be all about what she was bringing. That's what made it especially hard for her to find love. Maybe her standards were too high; perhaps the bar was too high. Either way, she wouldn't settle for just anybody. The man that captured her heart would have to be remarkable.

Chapter 38

Tammy's face told the story of how she felt. Her tears kept flowing; her thoughts were on Ingrid. She kept seeing Ingrid in the casket. Her funeral had completed it all. Life was short and definitely not guaranteed. She tried to control her tears but just couldn't do it. She thought she had cried them all at the funeral. If she was feeling like this, she knew Cashmere was definitely distraught. She wanted to call her but decided not to do so. Instead, she would give her time to grieve and reach out to her later in the week.

Tammy took a ride. There was nothing like rolling through those country roads to take her mind off her problems. She headed to Bradley Bridge Road and took Route 10 to Centralia Road. Top-down, jazz playing, cruising through those tree-lined curves. This brought her back to reality. Being out there, rolling through the country. Seeing familiar places. She turned around and headed to River Road. Took River Road passing through Ettrick, crossing the bridge, and going to Petersburg. Her mind was clear. Tears had ceased to flow. She felt the need to get something to eat. She was close to Rico's; she thought she would call him to see if he was hungry.

Rico... Hey baby, how are you?

Tammy... I am good, baby. How are you?

Rico... Good, thanks. What are you up to?

Tammy... Just out for a drive. I am close to your spot. I was going to stop and get something to eat. Have you eaten yet?

Rico... Very nice. No, I haven't eaten yet. Would you like to go out to get something?

Tammy... Well, I was going to pick something up and come over. Is that cool with you?

Rico... Yeah, that's cool. Where were you thinking about stopping?

Tammy... Actually, I felt like cheating today. Instead, I thought about getting a big juicy burger, some onion rings, and maybe a shake. Does that sound good to you?

Rico... Well, if we will cheat. May as well go all out. Yeah, that sounds great. Make mine a double, please.

Tammy... All right, I'll be there in a little while.

Rico... Cool, thanks, baby. See you soon.

Tammy... You're welcome.

Rico had been looking at the engagement ring; he had to put it up before she arrived. First, he needed to hide it so she wouldn't find it. Also, he needed to remember where he put it. Next, he put a bottle of Moscato in the refrigerator; he knew she would eventually want some. He always ensured he had enough Moscato on hand, just for these occasions.

About thirty minutes later, Tammy pulled up in the driveway. The front door was open, and she called for him, "Rico." Rico came to the door with a big smile on his face. "Hey, baby," he said as he opened the door for her. He took the bags of food from her. Went to the kitchen and placed the bags on the table. Before she could say another word. He pulled her close to him and planted a kiss on her lips. "It's good to see you, baby." "Good to see you too, Rico." He pulled her chair out for her and pushed it in after she sat down. She opened the bags after he sat down. Pulling out his food first, she placed it in front of him. She pulled her food out too. They both looked down, knowing they would somehow have to work all this food off. The grease had run down their fingers when they finished eating those burgers. Those were the best burgers! The messy, gooey, grease-dripping ones. They both just sat back, satiated from the food. Soon the itis would set in, and that would be all she wrote. Rico grabbed the trash, placed it in the bags, then threw the bags in the trash can. "Come on, baby, let's go outside for a while. It's a nice day out." They sat on the chaise together. All they could do was lay in each other's arms. They were too full to do anything else but lay there. About forty-five minutes later, Tammy woke up to Rico snoring. She tried to ease off the chaise without waking him up. As soon as she got up, he stirred. When he woke up, he saw her walking into the house. When she returned, she had a glass of Moscato and a Modelo for him. "Here you go, baby." "Thank you, Tammy. I really appreciate it." She sat back down beside him, toasting each other. He knew that she needed this time with him. He needed this time too. All he could think about was how and when he would propose to her and what would happen if she ever found out about the dirt he contacted Crush about. He had to make sure she never found out about that. Although, he couldn't totally control that. He hoped that R.J. and Crush would take the secret to their graves. He knew Crush wouldn't say anything because he would implicate himself. He trusted R.J. with everything, so he didn't think he would say anything. One never knows, though. He knew that today wasn't the time to reflect on all that; it kept creeping into his mind. Every time he looked at Tammy, his heart sank in his chest. He didn't want to lose what they had worked so hard to have together. He knew she wouldn't understand why he did it. She wasn't about that. In fact, it was that life that had encouraged her to become a lawyer. There was a side to him she didn't know and hopefully would never understand. "Rico? Where are you? You seem so far away." "Sorry, baby, just basking at the moment. It's good having you here with me." He hoped that she was okay with that answer. Hopefully, she wouldn't ask any more questions. He knew he couldn't keep lying to her about it. His heart wouldn't let him, but he could never tell her the truth.

Chapter 39

Cashmere had been through a box of tissues over lying Ingrid to rest. Lil Ingrid was crying, so she had to get herself together. She dried her tears, put on her big girl panties, and went to take care of her. She needed her bottle and needed changing again. She went into the room to check her diaper. Luckily, she was in the clear with that. She warmed up a bottle when it was ready, sat on the couch, and fed her. Lil Ingrid sucked that bottle down like it was nothing. She placed her on her shoulder and tapped her back until she belched. She sat Lil Ingrid on her lap and bounced her up and down. Lil Ingrid smiled. She had Cashmere's heart already. This little gift from heaven could be the one to change Cashmere. To make her realize and live her life the way she should. She could make her put her life in perspective. Realize her issues and her flaws and hopefully strive to be a better Cashmere. While she was playing with Lil Ingrid, her phone rang.

Cashmere... Hello!

Simeon... Hey, Cashmere. You've been on my mind lately.

Cashmere... Is that so?

Simeon... Of course. Are you okay?

Cashmere... Yeah, I am okay. Thanks.

Simeon... Are you sure?

Cashmere... Well, I could be better. I am coming around, though.

Simeon... Good. Is there anything I can do to help you with that?

Cashmere... Not really. I think this is something I must do on my own, though. I appreciate you asking, though.

Simeon... No doubt Cashmere. I hope you know that I am here for you.

Cashmere... That's good to know. How are things going with you? How is the music going?

Simeon... Things are well with me; the music is going well too. I have been in the studio working on some hotness.

Cashmere... That's great. I would love to hear it sometime.

Simeon... Actually, I'm glad you said that. I will be in the VA. in two weeks. I would love to see you.

Cashmere... That would be cool. I would love to see you too. In fact, I think I need to see you.

Simeon... Now, I like the sound of that. Okay, I will be in town for a week; I have studio sessions in Richmond.

Cashmere... Great. We will definitely have to make time to see one another.

Simeon... That's why I am calling ahead of time. I know you are busy. I know you have a lot going on right now. So I didn't want to just pop up on you.

Cashmere... I appreciate that. I'll have to work something out with Lil Ingrid. Hopefully, Uncle Herbert can keep her for a little while.

Simeon... Sounds good. I would love to meet her. I bet she is just as beautiful as you are.

Cashmere... Oh, she is definitely a cutie. I would love for you to meet her too.

Simeon... Cool!

There was an awkward silence for a few moments.

Cashmere... It was great to hear your voice. Don't be a stranger.

Simeon... That wasn't my intention. I was giving you some time to deal with what you needed. I wanted to be there more for you, but I didn't want to be a bother.

Cashmere... You could never be a bother, but I understand.

Simeon... Okay, good. I will call you tomorrow then. Is that good?

Cashmere... Yeah, that sounds good. I look forward to it. Talk to you tomorrow.

Simeon... All right, tomorrow then. Goodbye.

Cashmere... Bye, Simeon.

They both hung up the phone. Cashmere felt good about talking to him. She had wondered about their relationship. She had been distant since everything had happened. She was glad Simeon understood.

Simeon had taken her mind off of Ingrid for the time being. For once, she actually felt good again. She felt a little bit of happiness while she was talking to him. There was just something about him that seemed to make everything right with her. Finally, she had something to look forward to. She would ensure he would have a great time when he got to Virginia. Deep down, she needed to have a great time too. She needed to regain her life; she needed to get back to being Cashmere. Simeon was just the person to help her with that too.

Lil Ingrid had fallen asleep in her arms. She carried her to her room and placed her in the crib. When she returned to the kitchen, she grabbed a glass and poured Moscato into it. She took a much-needed sip and proceeded to the living room. Grabbing the remote, she turned on the television. Another drink eased down her throat as she surfed the channels for something good to watch. Finally, she saw something that piqued her interest. She put the remote down and watched the show, taking another big sip of Moscato. When she finished the Moscato, she placed the glass on the table and laid down on the couch. As she lay there, her eyes got heavy. Before she knew it, sleep had befallen her. She was exhausted, and the wine had relaxed her considerably. Sleep was something she hadn't been used to getting lately.

About forty minutes later, she awoke to her phone ringing. She looked at it. Uncle Herbert was calling.

Cashmere... Hello

Uncle Herbert... Hey Cashmere, how are you?

Cashmere... I am well, Uncle Herbert. How are you?

Uncle Herbert... Are you sure you're okay? I haven't heard from you since the funeral. I was worried about you.

Cashmere... I know Uncle Herbert. I am sorry I haven't called you. I guess I have just been dealing with this whole thing.

Uncle Herbert... I understand. I have been doing the same thing. I tell you what, take a few more days off and return to work on Monday. We need to get back to business.

Cashmere... Okay, thanks. You are right; we must get things back to normal, or at least as usual as they can be.

Uncle Herbert... Exactly. Okay, I will check on you in a few days.

Cashmere... Thanks, Uncle Herbert. I love you.

Uncle Herbert... I love you too. Talk to you soon.

She hung up the phone, placed it on the table, and checked on the baby. Lil Ingrid was still sound asleep. Cashmere just stood there watching her sleep for a few moments. She looked so peaceful; it brought a smile to her face. She saw so much of Ingrid in her. It was like looking at Ingrid when she was a little baby. This was the first time she could think about Ingrid without weeping.

Chapter 40

Stephanie's mind was still reeling from last night's date with Caleb. He had proven to be very charming, confident, and witty. Her only regret was that she hadn't accepted the date sooner. Some time had passed since she had been interested in anyone, but now, she was possibly back in the dating game. Her thoughts were consumed by someone again. It felt good to be liked by the opposite sex again. After all that she had been through, this was what she now needed in her life. Someone to take her mind off of the things that bothered her most. Someone other than her girls and her parents to share something with. Possibly she was reading way too far into this, but if things were to work out with Caleb, it would be all right with her.

After fixing breakfast, she relaxed on the patio for a bit. The morning air was crisp and clean. There was a slight breeze to be felt every so often. She sat back and enjoyed the morning weather while thinking about her day plans. She knew that there would be a stop at the restaurant. Hopefully, she will see her girls later. She thought it would be nice to talk to Caleb too. She wouldn't call him, though; the next phone call was definitely on him. Hopefully, it wouldn't be too long before she heard from him again.

She was ready to ride to the restaurant when she finished washing and putting away her dishes. When she got there, breakfast was being served in a half-filled restaurant. That was fine with her considering that Rains had only been open for a few hours. She went to her office to look over some paperwork. She was shuffling through some of her files and found a letter that Matthius had left her. She thought she had given all the evidence to Caleb. Unfortunately, this one had been missed. It wouldn't matter now since Matthius serving a ten-year bid for stalking and attempted murder. She quickly shredded the note. It was as if she was bringing closure to the case once and for all. Putting it in her past, out of her life for good. It was time for her to remove the harmful elements from her life and replace them with positive aspects.

Caleb would hopefully be one of the positive elements for her. She spent about an hour on her paperwork, then it was off to the kitchen to meet with the chef. Today she wanted to introduce a new item to the menu. She hoped that this meal would add a little something extra to the menu. It was a Caribbean jerk chicken and rice dish she hoped would not disappoint. She had been researching and making this dish for over two months. This recipe would be sheer perfection. Today, she would teach the chef how to prepare her version for tonight's special. It would definitely be featured on her menu if it was a success. The chef watched her prepare the dish, and they both tasted it. The flavors seemed to marry one another. It was a very appealing and fulfilling dish. Now, it was his turn to make it. Again, she watched him as he prepared it as she had prepared it. The final result was just as good as her dish. Stephanie was more than pleased with his Caribbean jerk chicken and rice dish. She instructed him to add it as a special for tonight's dinner. He was just as delighted to add the plate as she was. High fives between them were heard by the kitchen staff.

After adding the dish, she took a ride over to Club Char-Les-Manze. It had been a time since she had been there. She practically grew up in that club. Her parents were members back in the day. Now, she was so busy with life; that something consumed her with getting ahead. She sat at the bar and ordered a beer when she got there. Soon some familiar faces showed up. Stephanie engaged in conversation with them. They reminisce over the past. Talked about her new restaurant, her cruise, and life. By the time she looked up, two hours had passed. It was time for her to get home. She had a most enjoyable day. Now it was time to call it a night. Going to the club was a great idea. She got to see many people she hadn't seen in quite a while. It brought her back to a part of her childhood she was fond of. The only thing that would have made it better is if her girls had been there. By the time she got home, the sun was setting. She pulled into the garage, walked into the house, threw her keys on the table, and sank into her comfy couch. She had been out all day; all she wanted was to lay on the sofa and relax.

Chapter 41

Tammy... Hey baby, what are you doing?

Rico... Just getting in. You?

Tammy... The same. What did you do today?

Rico... I went to the cafe and helped, then met up with R.J. What did you do?

Tammy... It was a day from hell at work. I had a client that fell apart on the stand today. It was as if she had forgotten everything we discussed before the trial.

Rico... Was it that bad?

Tammy... It was just horrible. Unbelievable!

Rico... So what are you going to do now?

Tammy... I have no choice but to salvage what's left of the case. Hopefully, there is still a chance for us to win it.

Rico... Babe, if anybody can do it, you can. Do the damn thing!

Tammy... I know that's right, baby. Well, I won't keep you any longer. I want to see you, baby.

Rico... It's all good. I want to see you too, baby. Let's get together tomorrow after work. Maybe have a drink or something.

Tammy... Sounds good. Text me when and where, and I will meet you.

He always got excited when he knew he would see her. They had been dating for a while, and she still excited him. He was like a kid in a candy store when he was with her. She made him come alive and gave him some purpose.

Her excitement piqued. Rico made her heart sing every time she spoke to him. Yet, when she saw him, she also came alive. He was all that was ever wanted in a man. All that she desired in a man.

Rico grabbed a glass, dropped two rocks in it, and poured some Tennessee Honey, two fingers deep. Before he took a sip, he lit a Connecticut-wrapped cigar and dipped the tip in the Jack. He puffed and let the Jack-flavored smoke roll out his mouth. It had been a long time since he'd enjoyed a good cigar. Taking a sip of the Jack just made the cigar taste even better. He deemed this cigar as a pre-celebration for his proposal to Tammy.

Then he thought, what if she didn't accept his proposal? What if she says no? Did she feel the same way for him as he thought for her? Suddenly his confidence was diminishing slightly. Maybe he was being too presumptuous. There was only one way to find out: to ask her. He would let her decide whether he would be happy or disappointed. Hopefully, it wouldn't be the latter. If not, then there would be problems for them going forward. He took another look at the ring. A smile eased on his face. He knew that it was a stunning piece. He also knew that she would love it too! Or at least he hoped she would. One moment his confidence was definitely there; the next, he wasn't too sure. It wasn't until he had thought about proposing to her that doubt crept into the picture. Could it be that he knew what went down at the club could come back to haunt him? Not only could it, but if it did, it would ruin everything between them.

Rico... Let's do that little restaurant on the corner by your office. Let's say about 6pm.

Tammy... Okay, cool. Sounds good. I can't wait to see you, baby!

Rico... Neither can I. I have something for you too.

Tammy... What do you have for me, baby?

Rico... These lips to kiss yours with.

Tammy... Sweet but a little corny, babe.

Rico... Whatever, I will see you tomorrow.

Rico... All right, cool. I'll talk to you tomorrow, baby.

Tammy... All right. Good night Rico.

Rico... Good night, baby.

Tammy placed the phone down on the couch. Rico could be so sweet sometimes; she felt lucky to have him. He was indeed her everything. Excitement coursed through her body. The more she thought about seeing

Rico, the more excited she got. They both had been so preoccupied lately that they had had little time to spend together. Rico had a lot going on at the club, and Tammy had pulled some late nights at work. The case was taking a toll on her. She very much needed some Rico time! Missing being in his arms. The smell of his cologne when he stood near her. The way he made her feel when he touched her. Her thoughts were taking her places she enjoyed. Again, it had been some time since they had spent together. She needed him; she knew he needed her too. Soon they would enjoy one another again, the way it was meant to be.

Chapter 42

Char was hard at work on her new clothing line. Things had really taken off for her line. The desire for her fashion had proven to be much better than she expected. Her fans were very receptive to it. This would prove to be a great segue from modeling for her. Her heart was happy again. This had been something she had dreamed of for quite some time now. She had successfully placed her line in all the major stores. Now she was preparing for a fashion show showcasing her hard work. This fashion show was all about her. She was the featured designer. This is what designers look forward to, having designs featured in front of the fashion world. She had to be in New York in two days to prepare for the show. Everybody in the fashion world would be in Manhattan to catch a glimpse of her designs. She needed everything to be perfect. This was the night that could make or break her. There couldn't be any foul-ups or mistakes. She needed to make sure that all the clothing was ready to go. She had instructed her assistants to complete everything, but she felt she needed to double-check. This was her name; this was her reputation. This was her dream from the start. She couldn't leave any of it to chance. She had to be confident that everything was perfect! She caught up with her assistants, who were hard at work getting the line ready for shipping. Just as she had expected, there was an entire rack of clothing that still needed preparation. She had an hour left before the courier would be there to pick everything up. The dress was shipped overnight, so everything would be ready for her arrival. Luckily, they could get the clothing situated just before the couriers arrived. She breathed a massive sigh of relief when they left with the dress. She knew there would be many more sighs of relief over the next few days. She and her assistants were to fly out bright and early tomorrow morning. They would be in New York before noon. She wanted to be there a day early, just in case of unforeseen issues. She was about to do big things in the Big Apple this weekend. By the time she was done, she would hopefully be a household name, as far as designers go! From My Mother's Closet would be on the minds and lips of everybody in the fashion industry. She hoped that this time next week, her phone would blow up with orders for her line. She was reaching out to the big ballers of the industry this weekend. Hopefully, this will cement her legacy.

The morning came a lot quicker than she had expected. She had only laid down a few hours ago. Looking at the clock, it said 6:45am. She had overslept by half an hour. Her flight was due to leave at 8:30am; she still needed to get ready. Her limo was scheduled to arrive in forty minutes. This would be the fastest shower in history. Before she left, there wouldn't be any time for the breakfast she was looking forward to making. If she was lucky, she could get something on the way to the plane. It would have to be something quick. The one thing she had spoiled herself since she stopped modeling was having a good breakfast before starting her day. That was something she had missed out on while she was modeling. That lifestyle was hectic; she didn't have time to even think about eating, much less make it. Designing her own clothes kept her busy, but she had more control over what she did and when. She had time to think about what she wanted to accomplish. She was finally in control of her own destiny. She was the decider of just how far her dreams would take her. She and GOD!

Chapter 43

Caleb walked into his office to a mountain of paperwork. He sat in his chair and thought, will this ever end? The case files were piling up, and the cases were becoming harder and harder to solve. It was like the criminals were really becoming masterminds. Finally, he clicked on his mouse, which opened his email. That's when a smile crossed his face.

Stephanie... Good morning; I hope you are having a great day so far!

Caleb... I am having a great day now.

Stephanie... That's good to know. I had fun the other night.

Caleb... Great to know. I had fun too. We should get together and do it again.

Stephanie... Yeah, we should. That would be wonderful. What did you have in mind?

Caleb... Well, I thought we could go for a walk.

Stephanie... A walk?

Caleb... Yeah, a walk. You walk, right?

Stephanie... Of course I walk. I just haven't done it as a date.

Caleb... See, I am introducing you to new things. Don't worry, I got you.

Stephanie... Oh, I am not worried! I have a good feeling about you.

Caleb... Is that so?

Stephanie... Yes, that is so.

Caleb... That is great to know.

Stephanie... Please don't take my feelings for granted. I rarely do this sort of thing.

Caleb took a moment before he responded. He knew she had just gotten real!

Caleb... I won't. I understand how you feel. I have been there myself.

Stephanie... I hope you mean that because if you ever take me for granted, I am out the door.

He thought she must have gone through a thing or two. But then, she just made it serious.

Caleb... Well, I guess you'll just have to stick around to find out, won't you?

Stephanie... We'll just have to see about that, won't we?

For some reason, the vibe had changed. What was going on in her mind? Why was she throwing out mixed signals? Had he said something wrong and didn't know it?

Caleb... I hope so!

He waited for a response; there wasn't one. She had stopped talking to him. Damn, what had he said that would make her act this way? Right when he thought he was winning her over. Something had taken a turn for the worse. He wasn't sure what it was, but it was something! Unfortunately, he would have to worry about that a little later on. For now, these cases were calling his name. Although his focus would not be 100%, he still needed to handle his business. He reviewed several files, trying his best to focus. Unfortunately, his mind kept going back to Stephanie. He made a few phone calls to follow up on some leads. When he was done, he delved back into the files. This time he forced his thoughts of her out of his mind. Or at least he thought he had until he realized he had already read the same sentence three times. Dammit, all he could think about was her. He didn't need that right now. He needed to focus on his work before another innocent victim lost their life. His phone buzzed with a text.

Stephanie... I hope so too.

She finally replied. Had he been worried for nothing? He would soon find out that was for sure.

Caleb... That's good to know.

Stephanie... Why do you say that?

Caleb... You seemed to be bothered by something earlier. I wasn't sure if things were still good.

Stephanie... Things are still good with us. I was just letting you know what's real.

Caleb... What brought that on?

Stephanie... Just setting the ground rules.

Caleb... Is that so?

Stephanie... You have to put it all out there so there aren't any issues down the line. If you know what I will and won't deal with, you won't make those mistakes later.

Caleb... Oh, is that so? Well, since you brought up the do's and don't. Here is my biggest pet peeve. Don't be late; I don't want to have to wait on you.

Stephanie... Okay, got it. Maybe I shouldn't have opened that door.

Caleb... It's all good. Now we both know what's up.

Stephanie... That is true! Changing the subject, when are we going on that walk?

Caleb... I thought we could go on Sunday. I know a nice spot I think you would like.

Stephanie... Sunday sounds good.

Caleb... Great, I will pick you up around noon. Is that cool?

Stephanie... Noon sounds good.

Caleb... Wear something comfortable.

Stephanie... I will do just that.

Caleb... Cool, see you Sunday!

Sunday couldn't come around soon enough for Stephanie. She wanted to see him again; he excited her with his charming, charismatic style. Even though he tried to take her on a walk. That was definitely the most uncommon date someone had ever invited her on. Usually, dinner, a movie, or even a club, but never a walk. We would see just what he has in store. Hopefully, it was someplace nice with incredible scenery. Hell, for all she knew, he wanted to walk around the block. She could tell he was more romantic than that. She was sure he was planning something to sweep her off her feet. At least, she hoped so anyway. Caleb had that swagger about him that intrigued her. She wanted to know just what he was up to. Just what he had in store for her.

When Sunday came, she sprung out of bed at about 9:30 in the morning. It was so hard to contain her excitement. She made herself some coffee and two boiled eggs. She didn't want to overeat, just in case; Caleb tried to surprise her with a meal. She got her clothes ready the night before. All she had to do was put on her make-up and wait for him to arrive. She still had some time, so she sat on the deck for a bit while having breakfast. It was a beautiful morning. There was a slight breeze in the air. People were already out and about enjoying the day. Soon she would join them to enjoy her day. She finished her coffee and eggs. It was time for her to get dressed. He would be there in about an hour. After she was ready, she poured herself a glass of Moscato to relieve her nervousness. She didn't want him to see how excited he made her feel. She couldn't have that going to his head. He might think he was the man or something. She had to continue to play it cool. Let him be the one to express his excitement first. The game was too new to let him think he was all that.

Chapter 44

Simeon exited the plane in Richmond. When he gathered his bags and walked out front, he waited for Cashmere for about 20 minutes. She didn't hear her alarm and had overslept. She was a good hour away from the airport. She texts him apologetically.

Cashmere... I am so sorry, Simeon, I overslept. I just woke up. It will take me about an hour to get there.

Simeon... Oh damn, don't worry about picking me up then. I will catch a cab. I'll call you later on after I finish up at the studio.

Cashmere paused before she replied. She wanted to see him before he went to the studio. No telling what time she would see him now. Damn, she had messed up badly.

Cashmere... Okay, I am sorry about this. I hope you have a good session at the studio. See you soon, I hope!

Simeon... Okay, thanks. I'll text you later!

Cashmere... Okay.

Disappointment just sort of lingered on his face for some seconds. He hadn't seen Cashmere in about a month, and she couldn't even pick him up on time. Grant it, she was going through some things, but maybe he wasn't as important to her as he thought he was or as she eluded. He could have caught the cab over to her place, but he wanted to give her some time to think about this whole thing. Maybe it would help her remember just how she should feel about him. It was one thing to miss him because he was in New York, but to miss him while he was in her city, while he was so close to her, should make her think differently. When he got to the studio, he told his boy about her oversleeping. Rather than just talk about it, they poured two glasses of Hennessey. They went into the studio to capture that emotion on a track. Simeon took a sip, went to the booth, and waited for his boy to pull up the track. When the track played in his headphones, he hummed to it. When he finished the vocals, they were filled with emotion, filled with hurt. They oozed desire and heartbreak. Simeon laid into the lyrics like he had never laid into them before. By the time he ended the song, they knew they were on to something. Listening to it again, they added a little more to the ending. They wanted the finish to be spectacular. They wanted the song to resonate with the people who have gone through or are struggling with a real relationship. Simeon's voice was smooth, and his range was incredible. He had a way of delivering the lyrics like an artist that painted smooth, flowing brush strokes. This track was hot already, and they both knew it too! He had put his all on this track. He was definitely talking to Cashmere on this one. He wanted her to know just how he felt about her madness. He needed her to see they could have something great if she just came correctly! His boy played the track again. They listened to it several times. Simeon laid some solid harmonies. It made it even sexier. This track definitely spoke to Cashmere and would resonate with the ladies there. He was feeling this track. This could be the one right here. It could be that debut single that would put him in the game significantly!

His phone buzzed. He looked down at it; it was Cashmere texting.

Cashmere... Hey, I hope you are having a great session. Call me when you want me to come and get you!

He kind of laughed at the text. He would not respond anytime soon. She knew it pissed him off. Now she was trying to go out of her way to make it up to him. This time it would not be as easy. He would make her sweat it out for a minute! "Yo, Simeon, do you need a minute to respond to that text? I got levels I need to work on, anyway." "Nah, bruh, I'm good. She can wait!" A devilish smile crept on his face. He was being spiteful now. He wanted her to feel wrong about this bull she put him through. Hopefully, she will learn a lesson. He laughed cause he remembered he was talking about Cashmere. She definitely wouldn't learn from this. Or would she? He didn't have time to keep thinking about this. He put the phone down and got back to the music.

His boy was working on the levels, trying to get them right. The track played through the speakers; they both were bobbing their heads. "Simeon, you did the damn thing on that track. I think you might be onto something here." "Yeah, man, I am feeling it. Do you think it needs anything else? Does it have enough?" "Man, I think you did all you could on this one. Let me put my thing on it. I'll get the levels right and mix it down. We'll see what we have after that." "Cool! Do you want to hit more of this, Henny?" "Hell yeah, pour me another, my brother!" Simeon grabbed the Henny and poured more into their glasses. They raised their glasses "Cheers to a hit, my brother," Simeon said.

"I know that's right, my brother. Let's get this hit! Let's get this paper!" They were both feeling great about the track. Maybe he should thank Cashmere since his frustration with her fueled this masterpiece. He wanted to text her, call her and share this with her. But unfortunately, he was still a little frustrated with her. He wasn't ready to talk to her yet. When he spoke to her, though, he wanted her to be very sorry for not being there for him.

Moreover, he wanted her to think twice before she did anything like that again. He needed to be too essential for her to oversleep again. If not, then they couldn't be an item. She needed to step her game up if she would get with his program. It was time for him to put her up on his game! It was SIMEON time!

Chapter 45

Tammy was finishing up at the firm; it had been a day. Nothing had gone as it should. Everything that could go wrong at work went wrong. Although she loved her job, some days it was just too much for her to deal with. Hell, some days, it was too damn much for anybody to deal with. She turned her computer off, locked her files, and grabbed her coat and purse. She walked to the door, turned off the lights, and headed to the elevator. This place had consumed too much of her time today. It was time for some relaxation, wine, and hopefully some Rico! She got to the garage and hit the alarm on the ride. She sunk into the leather seats, started the car up, pulled off, and let the ride soothe her. Once she got home, she pulled off her shoes and poured herself a glass of Moscato. Headed to the bedroom, pulled her dress off, and lay on the bed in her panties and bra. She sipped on her Moscato; it eased through her body, relaxing all of her. She needed this. She picked up the glass again; there wasn't anything left. She had devoured the glass. She got up, went to the kitchen, grabbed the bottle, and returned to the bedroom. Laying on the bed and clicking the remote on the stereo. Some old-school rhythm and blues flowed through the speakers. That's right, it was that kind of night. This was a night she deserved. There wouldn't be any working from home tonight. She wouldn't even think about doing any such work. Tonight was for her only. Unless Rico somehow surprised her. That would make everything all better. She needed to see him. Needed to be close to him. Some of those Rico kisses all over her body would be great now. She yearned to feel his hands all over her. He knew just what to do to make her feel like a woman should feel. Her mind took her back to the last time they made love. He had ravished her body. Made her body tingle in places she hadn't tingled before. Rico always handled his business. She wanted him; she needed him. She wanted to feel him deep within her. She missed how he worshiped her body when they got hot and heavy. He took care of her, unlike any man had done before him. Her mind was taking her to places that made her wish that Rico was there now. If he were, he would take care of her. He would give her body the attention she needed. Make her forget all about her stressful work day. Why was she wishing, hoping that

Rico would just show up? She knew how to handle this. She picked up her phone.

Tammy... Hey, what are you doing?

Rico... Just getting in. What are you doing?

She took a picture of her in her bra and panties.

Tammy... This is what I am doing.

She sent him a picture of her lying on the bed.

Rico... Oh, I see. It looks like you might need company.

Tammy... Hurry, don't make me wait too long!

Rico... Say no more! I am on my way.

Tammy... I can't wait to see you, baby. I want you!

Rico... Be there soon!

Rico jumped in the shower to get the work day off of him. Once he finished, he dressed, got his keys, and headed over. His mind was on that pic she sent him the whole ride over. She looked good in her bra and panties. Her curves were hitting in all the right places.

What's more, is that he loved enjoying her. She took great care to make sure he was well taken care of. The perfume she wore always made him want her more.

When he pulled up, he couldn't get out of the car fast enough. He had closed the door and walked away. He turned around and noticed that the car was still running. Damn, she had his mind wide open. He couldn't help but laugh. He turned the car off and headed to the door. Before he could ring the bell, she opened the door. "Come on in, baby," she said, standing in her burgundy bra and panties. She placed a kiss on him that screamed, "You've been away from me too damn long!" She rubbed her hands up and down his back. He pulled her close to him. He let his hands slide down over her backside. She let out a soft moan to let him know that his touch was more than welcome. She pulled his shirt out of his jeans and ran her hand along his chest. "Damn baby, you feel so good. I have missed you," she said. He unfastened her bra, eased both straps, and let it fall to the floor. Her breasts were there for him to enjoy. Her nipples were at attention, yearning for his touch. He placed gentle kisses between her breasts. It had been a week since they had made love, and her body reacted to his lips being between them.

He picked her up and carried her to the bedroom. He laid her down and eased her panties off her. She had his undivided attention. She waited patiently for him to join her in the bed. As soon as he laid down, she got on top of him and kissed him all over. Damn, his body felt good to her. This was just what she needed to take her mind off her day. She placed kisses all over his chest. She could feel his hands rubbing down her back. The lower his hands traveled, the more excited she got. He was close to where she wanted his hands to be. She loved it when he caressed her backside. His hands were big and very strong. She couldn't get enough of his touch. He pulled her to him to place kisses on her sexy lips. She opened her mouth to receive his tongue. She could feel him rising beneath her. That was the feeling she was waiting for. She would feel him deep within her soon. He rolled her over in the bed and slowly lowered his body over hers. He was inches from touching her. He pressed his lips against hers, giving her another kiss that would send electricity through her body. She wanted him. Wanted him more than ever before. He slid down her body, kissing her breasts, stomach, and thighs. Her perfume was on point. Her lovely smell enticed him. "Come on, baby! I need you," she moaned softly. He looked down at her anticipating the goodness that was mere seconds away. He slid his hands down around her waist. He ran his fingers between her soft hair and brought her lips to his. She looked at him; she could hardly wait. He was ready, and so was she! He laid on top of her and eased himself inside her. She sighed a little. It had been almost too many days since she had taken him inside of her. He felt good to her. He was doing everything she needed him to do. She put her arms around his back, pulling him closer to her. He pleased her to no end. By the time they were done, they both were satiated. He had given her what she desired. She had given herself to him. Each time they made love just seemed to get better and better.

He had thought about reminding her they were supposed to meet at 6. He chose not to, though. This was much better than meeting at some bar. He pulled her close, and they fell asleep in each other's arms.

Chapter 46

When Char's private jet landed in Richmond, she was exhausted and excited. Finally, the fashion show was a grand success! Her From My Mother's Closet line was about to be the next hottest thing in the fashion world. Finally, Char had done it; she had accomplished what she set out to accomplish. Her line was about to be in every clothing store, in every fashion magazine, and on the lips of everybody who was anybody in the fashion industry. She was hot again. She had gone from a successful model to a successful fashion designer.

When the limo pulled up to her place, she was more than ready to go inside. What she needed now was a nice long, hot shower. After that, laying down and getting some much-needed rest was on the agenda. She would worry about unpacking her clothes later. She didn't want to think about the clothing line, her girls, or anything else. All she wanted was to close her eyes and catch up on some sleep. It was Char time now.

By the time her eyes opened again, it was morning. She had slept the night away uninterrupted. She jumped in the shower to wake up. There wasn't much on her agenda today. She would try to do as little as possible. After showering, she put on a satin robe and went into the kitchen to make herself a pot of coffee. That would be the drink of choice for the day, at least in the morning. She grabbed two slices of bread to make the toast. Char liked to prepare her toast in the oven. She would place four spots of butter, one in each corner.

When done, it was always so tasty. It added a little more than putting it in the toaster. It was a trick her mother showed her when she was a little girl. Char loved to watch her mother cook when she was growing up. It was one of her favorite things about spending time with her mother. Her mother was an excellent cook. Char is a great cook but not nearly as good as her mother was. Her mother had a way of taking the simplest ingredients and making a mouthwatering meal. That was something that her mother learned from her mother. They were three generations of culinary geniuses. When her toast and coffee were ready, she sat at the table and smiled. Looking at her toast, she couldn't help but think about her mother.

Thinking about her mother always brought a big ole smile because she had been close to her mother. They had a great bond. Her mother had been her rock. She was the one person she could talk to about anything. She would just hear her out. See, to her mother, she wasn't Char, the superstar; she was Char, the daughter. No matter how big she got in the world, she was still her mother's little girl. One thing that her mother had told her that stuck with her was, "If you didn't make a problem, there wouldn't be a problem!" That was a statement she lived her life by. Rather than creating problems, she created solutions. It was far easier to live your life with solutions rather than problems. It was something she always thought about, especially when she faced adversity.

Tears flowed down her face. It had been three years ago when she got that horrible phone call. Her mother had died in her sleep. Her heart had stopped in the middle of the night. It was a total surprise because her mother was the picture of perfect health. She remembered it like it was yesterday. She had been on a shoot in Bora Bora when she received the word. She chartered a jet and returned to Virginia to take care of all the arrangements. She couldn't hold back the tears. She thought about her mother every day, but the anniversary of her death was always the hardest for her. They always say that losing somebody close to you gets easier as time passes. To her, that was the farthest thing from the truth. It had been three years, and it wasn't getting any easier to deal with. In fact, it was getting harder to deal with. She couldn't sit down and talk to her mother about everything happening in her life. That was the roughest part: being unable to see, talk to, or hug her. Instead, she took comfort in knowing that her mother looked down on her and smiled. She had always wanted to make her mother proud of her. She knew she had accomplished that because her mother had told her that so many times before she journeyed. She missed that about her mother. She was so honest and wasn't scared to speak her mind. Char knew she was getting the most honest opinion when she spoke. Whether it was in her favor or not, it was sheer honesty in its purest form. When she finished her toast and coffee, she found she had craved another cup of joe. The blend was so flavorful that sometimes she would have several cups throughout the day. It wasn't often that she could just relax and drink coffee. Her schedule kept her so busy that relaxing had turned into a luxury.

Today though, she had promised herself that it would be a chilled day. All she would do was remember her mother, drink coffee and get her chill on. There wouldn't be any phone calls, text messages, emails, or visitors today. It was just going to be about her today. She checked her phone to see if she had received any calls or messages. Sure enough, there were already four calls and two messages. She smiled and just left the phone in her bedroom. She was determined to chill today; nothing would keep her from doing so. Her gate intercom buzzed. She looked at the camera and saw a courier van. "Yes, how may I help you?" "We have a package for a Char LesManze." "Okay, I'll buzz you in. Follow the driveway until you reach the house."

"Will do, thanks." What on earth could it be? She wasn't expecting anything? A few minutes later, the doorbell rang. She opened the door, signed for the package, and closed the door. She opened the box; it was an official invitation to the Fashion Industry Awards show in Los Angeles. Someone nominated Char for a *"Newcomers Award."* This had turned out to be a great day. She knew that her line was doing well, but to be nominated for an award solidified her confidence and efforts. Okay, enough of the coffee. It was time to celebrate a little. She broke out the Moscato.

Chapter 47

It was Friday, and the weekend had rolled in. Quitting time was now for Stephanie. So much had happened; so many great things had transpired. The one thing she thought was that it had been some time since she and her girls had gotten together. Everybody was so busy living their lives. She needed to change that up, at least for a night. So she grabbed her phone and sent out a group text.

Stephanie... Hey ladies, I hope everybody is doing well. It has been a minute since we have been out.

Tammy... Hey ladies, she's right. We need to get together!

Char... That would be great!

Cashmere... I would love to, but I have a guest in town.

Tammy... Girl, you can't get away for two hours?

Char... Hell, bring him with you.

Stephanie... I know that's right.

Cashmere... I could do that too. Where and when are we talking about?

Stephanie... Well, tomorrow is the first anniversary of our trip to The Crib. I thought we could go there again to celebrate.

Tammy... Oh, that is a great idea. Let me see if Rico can get us the VIP section again.

Cashmere... Now that's what I'm talking about. Let's get more of those chocolate-covered strawberries too.

Char... Cashmere, you are so damn funny.

Cashmere... What? You know you were thinking the same thing.

Stephanie... Hell, I know I was. Hopefully, he can get that same spread again. That night was off the chain.

Tammy... I will do my best to get him to hook it up like he did last time.

Cashmere... Girl, you better put it on him, so he takes care of us!

Stephanie... I know that's right!

Tammy... Let's plan on getting there around 9:30. I'll let y'all know what Rico says.

Cashmere... Cool.

Stephanie... Okay.

Char. Sounds great. Thanks, Tammy.

Tammy had just gotten in from work. She was expecting Rico to come through the door at any moment. Grabbed a glass of Moscato and went to the bedroom to change into something more comfortable. When she was done, she heard the door open. "Babe, are you here?" "Yeah, I'm in the bedroom." A few seconds later, he appeared in the bedroom. "What an appropriate place for us to meet," Rico said as he walked over to her. He placed his hands on her face and gave her one of those great kisses she loved. "How was your day, baby?" "It was great, baby, and yours?" "It was a day. I finished talking to the girls. Do you know what tomorrow is?" "I know what tomorrow is, baby. It is the anniversary of our first date." Tammy just smiled. "Yeah, it is. I am so glad you remembered." She had been so excited about talking to her girls that it had totally slipped her mind about their anniversary. Damn, how could she forget about it? "So, what did your girls have to say?" "Oh, they wanted to get together tomorrow night at The Crib." She waited to see what he would say. He paused for a few seconds. It had dawned on him she might have forgotten about their anniversary. "You know what? That sounds like a plan. Do you want me to get the VIP section for y'all?" He let her off the hook. He figured they would have plenty more time to celebrate their anniversary. It relieved her that he didn't make a big deal about her forgetting about it. "Baby, that would be nice. We would appreciate it!" "Great, I'll make it happen, baby. You know I would do anything to make my baby happy!" Tammy wasn't sure if he meant that or if it was a dig for her not remembering. Either way, she would make the best of it because she didn't want to argue about anything right now. All she wanted to do was enjoy time with her girls and Rico. She would make sure she made it up to him!

Cashmere was dealing with the loss of Ingrid a little better. Times were still hard for her, but she took one day at a time. Lil Ingrid was growing so much. She was just so damn adorable. Simeon was helping her get back to being herself. Although, she had pissed him off by not picking him up from the airport. She knew that it would be all good when they met up. He worked on his music, but she knew he also needed to see her. Besides, their relationship always seemed to have an issue or two that made it more interesting. He would call soon, and she would pick him up, then it would be on. She had spoken with uncle Herbert; he was on board with watching Lil Ingrid, so she wouldn't have to divert her attention away from Simeon. There was a knock on her door. When she opened it, she saw Simeon. "Hey, I thought you would call me when you were ready." "I finished early, and I didn't want to bother you, so I got a ride here. Is that okay?" "Yeah, that's fine. Why wouldn't it be?" It was clear that Simeon still had a slight frustration towards her. "Good! No reason, just making sure." She showed him to the living room. "How did your session go?" "It was great. We worked on some hot tracks. I feel great about it." "That's great. Can I hear some of it?" "Not right now. It isn't finished yet, and I rarely let people hear my stuff until it is ready." "Oh, so I am people now?" Simeon wasn't sure how she meant that, so he stuck to his guns. "That includes everybody. Don't take it personally. If it's not ready, it can't be heard." She noticed the seriousness in his voice and decided not to press it. That was something uncharacteristic of her. She loved a good challenge. I guess she figured that she had already pushed his buttons earlier. She would give him a break for now. "Would you like something to drink?" "Yes, that would be great." "Okay, I'll be right back." He sat on the couch, turned on the television, and waited for her to return. He was flipping through the channels when she came back with the drinks. Moscato for her and a nice cold beer for him. "Thank you," he said as she passed it to him. She plopped down on the couch next to him. Her perfume brought back the memory of the last time they were together. "Do you want to go out tonight," she asked. "What did you have in mind?" "Well, my girls and I are going to "The Crib" tonight. I was hoping that you would join us." "You know what, I probably shouldn't do all that. You hang with your girls. I will work on some music until you get back. I have some lyrics that I need to get down, anyway." "Really? Are you serious?" "Very much so." Okay, he was tripping now. Cashmere wasn't feeling his response. "Okay, that's cool too. I won't be gone too long." "It's all good. I know you've been going through a lot lately. I totally understand. I will be here when you get back." She laid against his chest, hoping he would change his mind and go with her.

Char had her outfit all planned for tonight. She was more than ready to step out with her girls. She'd been about business for so long that she had forgotten how to have a good time. But she needed this right now. She needed to let her hair down a little. Her girls were just the ones to get her back in the groove. Her life had been so serious lately. Nothing but work, work, work. She hadn't had time for anything other than that. So she was looking forward to getting out, especially when she got to hang with her girls. The last time they went to The Crib, it was a blast. The whole VIP treatment that Rico hooked up was on point. Not that Char wasn't used to the entire VIP treatment, it was more like she wasn't used to doing it with her girls. When she got that treatment, it was mostly when she was out of town or out of the country. There had only been a few times that she got to do the whole VIP thing with her girls. But, she enjoyed it every time too.

Char had put on her clothes and was ready to head out to meet her girls. Tammy had already called and told her they were on their way. When she got there, Rico had the whole VIP thing on lock. They laced the tables with strawberries, chocolates, orange juice, cranberry juice, the usual liquors they all loved, and the Moscato. He even had security posted to ensure no one who wasn't part of the crew entered. Stephanie and Cashmere were the next to arrive. R.J. showed them over to the tables. He nodded at the security guard, and he allowed them to enter.

Char, Cashmere, and Stephanie hugged. It had been some time since they all had been together. Tammy and Rico strolled in a few minutes later; she was all smiles. She ran straight to the girls. "Hey ladies, how is everybody tonight," Tammy shouted. "We good girl, how are you," Cashmere said. "Give me a hug Tammy. I haven't seen you in a minute," Char said. The deejay had the music pumping already. Rico was making his rounds around the club, ensuring everything was good to go before he went to hang out with the girls.

The whole anniversary thing was still on his mind. He was trying to get through it, but it weighed heavily. I guess he realized that just maybe their relationship wasn't as meaningful to her as it was to him. He never would have forgotten about their anniversary. Moreover, he didn't think she would have ever done that either. Anyway, he continued to check on everything. He glanced at the VIP table, and the girls were immersed in conversation, giggles, and laughter. He couldn't help but think she was happy when she was with her girls. They were made for one another, indeed were a sisterhood with a bond. Tammy looked up and noticed him watching them. She smiled at him and mouthed, "I love you, baby!" He smiled and mouthed the exact words back to her. She smiled and watched him as he headed to the office. As he walked away, she felt slightly disappointed in herself for not remembering their anniversary. Damn, it was their first anniversary, and she didn't even realize it. She wondered what must go through his mind about her. "Tammy, Tammy, Tammy!" She faintly heard a voice calling her name. "Tammy, where are you, girl? Come back to us," Char said.

Chapter 48

"What? I'm here, I'm here," Tammy said. "Girl, you were in another world. Char was talking to you, and you didn't even realize it," Stephanie said. "I'm sorry, I had something on my mind. I'm good now, though." "What's on your mind Tammy," Cashmere said. "Well, I think I may have messed up tonight." "How is that? What did you do," Char said. "Tonight is also Rico and my first anniversary. I sort of forgot about it." "Oh, damn. Hold on, did he remember," Cashmere said. "Yeah, he did." "Yeah, you messed up home, girl. What are you doing here with us? You should be with your man," Cashmere said with a smirk on her face. "We haven't all been out in quite some time. I wanted to catch up." "You better make it up to him, that's for sure," Stephanie said. "I know, I know. I will do just that!" R.J. walked over to see how the girls were getting along. "Can I get anything for you, ladies?" "Do you have any pineapples," Cashmere asked? "Yeah,

I believe we have some in the kitchen. I'll be right back." R.J. smiled and went to the kitchen. "Damn Cashmere, you don't think they did enough? They laid out quite a spread for us," Char said. "Look, Char, didn't he ask us if we needed anything?" "Yeah, he did, but let's not take advantage." Cashmere shot her a look that said, "*back off, chic.*" Char shot her a look right back, saying, "don't *get to tripping.*" There it was, the girl's first little tiff for the evening. No outing was complete without them having one. Rico eased on into the VIP section; he sat down right beside Tammy. "Beautiful, how are you this evening?" She smiled and leaned into him. "I am fine handsome! How are you?" He leaned in and kissed her on the cheek. "That's how I'm doing, baby!" She smiled. "Get a room," Cashmere shouted with a smile. They all laughed loudly. Rico dipped a strawberry in some chocolate and gave it to Tammy. R.J. returned to the table with the pineapple that Cashmere had asked for. Cashmere thanked him and looked at Char, sticking her tongue out. "Whatever, Cashmere," Char said as she smiled.

The deejay was calling all couples to the floor. It was time to play "Let's Get Sexy." He would play several slow songs in a row. The sexier the dances were, the longer they would last on the floor. If the judges didn't think it was sexy, they would tap the guy on the shoulder for you to leave the floor. "Come on, baby, let's go," Tammy said. She grabbed Rico's hand, and they went out to the dance floor. The slow groove emanated from the speakers. Men pulled their ladies close to them. Bodies slowly moved from side to side.

Hands rubbed up and down backs. They were really getting into it. Tammy's hands were running up and down Rico's back. He was spinning her, dipping her, kissing her. Finally, the judges tapped two couples on the shoulder, they exited the floor. There were only three couples left. The other two couples were going for theirs too. One couple even broke out in a slow, sexy salsa. "Oh damn, they are doing the damn salsa," Cashmere said. "I don't blame them. I think the salsa is a very sexy dance," Char said. "Yeah, it is," Stephanie agreed. Cashmere refreshed her vodka and cranberry; she took a piece of pineapple and placed it in the glass. She took a sip while she watched Rico and Tammy do their thing on the dance floor.

"They really look good together, don't they," Stephanie said. "Yeah, they definitely look good together. Rico is so good for her. I can't remember when I saw her happier," Char said. "It is a trip she forgot about their anniversary and came out with us," Cashmere said. "I can't believe she did that, though. Rico must be frustrated with her," Stephanie said. "I bet, but he is doing a great job of pretending it doesn't bother him," Char said as she watched him spin Tammy again. "You know what, maybe we should leave and let them have the table to themselves to celebrate," Stephanie queried. "And let all this good booze go to waste. You must be crazy," Cashmere said matter-of-factly. Stephanie just laughed at Cashmere.

They were down to two couples on the dance floor. It was just then that Rico felt a tap on his shoulder. "I guess that's it for us, baby." "It's okay. I was getting thirsty anyway." They walked over to the table; Rico poured her some Moscato to quench her thirst.

"What's going on over here, ladies," Rico said. "We're just hanging out and having a great time. How are you doing, Mr. Rico" Cashmere said. The girls wanted to wish them both a happy anniversary, but they were unsure if it was a good idea. They didn't want to make things any worse between them. Rico seemed to have a good time right now. He was definitely playing the game well. Tammy wasn't sure if the whole thing bothered him or not. She was just riding it out. Eventually, she would find out. That's for sure. If he didn't seem upset, would that mean he didn't care? She knew he cared about her, but did he care about their anniversary? Did she care about their anniversary? For some people, it was just another day. Some couples celebrate their love every day, while others celebrate once a year. She wondered which couple they were. She hoped that they were not the latter. Either way, she was happy to have him as her man.

The club was jumping, and people were everywhere. Drinks were flowing around the table. The VIP section was the place to be; R.J. brought more pineapples, strawberries, and chocolate to the table. Cashmere was pouring the next round for everybody. Tammy was watching her too because everybody knew that Cashmere likes to pour heavy drinks. It was all good, though. Tonight was a celebration. They hadn't hung out together in a minute; everybody had been busy doing their own thing. It was time to let their hair down, so to speak. Maybe that was why Rico wasn't tripping. Perhaps he understood just how much Tammy needed this right now. Hell, deep down, all that mattered to him was her happiness. As long as she was happy, he was good to go. If she was displeased, he would surely make her happy.

Chapter 49

Stephanie heard his car pull up. She could hardly contain herself. She tried her best not to run to the door. The wait for him to ring the doorbell seemed like an eternity. Finally, the doorbell rang, and she tried to take as much time as possible to get to the door. When she opened it, he was standing there with a big smile. "Hello, how are you, Caleb?" "I am well, and you?" "I am well, thanks. Come in." As Caleb walked by her, she got a whiff of his cologne. His smell lingered there for her to enjoy for a few more seconds. She hugged him and inhaled another breath of him. Damn, he smelled good to her. She was ready to say, "forget this whole walking thing."

"Are you ready?" "Oh yes, sure. Let's go." She followed him out to his car, and he opened her door. When she got in, she reached over and opened his door. That brought a little smile to his face. He knew that most women didn't do that sort of thing. He backed out of the driveway, got on the freeway, and drove to Pocahontas State Park. "Pocahontas State Park is one of my favorite places. My parents used to bring me here when I was a little girl" "I love coming here too. There is a nice little path I want you to see."

He drove deeper into the park. Soon he parked his car in front of a cabin. He got out and walked around the back of the vehicle. Opening her door, he extended his hand for her to take. She had been to the park many times before but had never seen this part of the park. They walked into the cabin, grabbed a backpack, then went out the back door. "Caleb, whose cabin is this? What are we doing here?" "The cabin belongs to the park. It used by the rangers." "How do you have access to it?" "Well, my brother is a park ranger. Sometimes I help at the park, so I can access it."

"Okay, got it. So where are we going now?" "You'll see. Come with me." "I don't really go in the woods with strange men. Can I trust you?" "If you didn't think you could trust me, you wouldn't be here." Stephanie looked at him. She wasn't sure how to respond to his comment. She knew that he was right, though. "Would you like water," he asked. "You know what, I am a little thirsty. Yes, I will have water." He opened the backpack and pulled out some water for both of them. He opened her bottle and handed it to her. "Thank you so much, Caleb," she said as she took the water from him. "You are welcome." Stephanie took a sip, and a drop of water ran down her neck slowly. He placed his finger along the water and wiped it off her. He didn't have a clue how excited that simple touch made her. Her body tingled. If only she knew him well enough to take him right there. She couldn't, though. As much as she wanted him, she couldn't give herself to him yet. She had to get to know him better. Had to make sure he was the right one for her. It had been a time since she had been intimate with a man. Her body was telling her it was time. Her mind was telling her it was too soon for all that.

He reached for her hand, she accepted, and they walked towards the woods. Her hand felt very soft. He was happy to have her touching him. They walked deeper and deeper down the path. Before she knew it, they walked out, and suddenly there was an opening. What she saw then was beyond breathtaking. She couldn't believe that this was still Pocahontas State Park. Her eyes scanned all around, taking in all the beauty before her. "This is unbelievable!" "I wanted you to see something just as beautiful as you!" She smiled and was just in awe of the scenery. "Thank you so much, but nothing could ever be as beautiful as this." "I beg to differ. You are far more beautiful than this could ever be." She smiled as she looked at the cascading water running down the lush green rolling hills into the lake. "Stephanie, this place is exceptional, and I wanted to share it with you. I have never brought anybody up here, but I wanted you to see it. I wanted you to experience it with me." "Why is that?" "Because I wanted you to know just how beautiful I think you are. I think this place is special, but there is nothing on this earth that is more special than you." She pulled him close to her and kissed him on the lips. He received her kiss with blissful enjoyment. Her lips were soft. They were pressing against him in a way that begged him not to stop. She let her kiss linger on his lips, hands rubbing his back. His hands were on both sides of her face. She could tell he wanted to pull her closer, but she was already as close as she could get to him. Which she rather enjoyed! His body pressed up against hers, and smelling his cologne sent her mind to another place. She envisioned pushing him to the ground, getting on top of him. Kissing his lips intently. Rubbing her body against his, letting him touch her where ever he liked. Smelling his cologne, kissing his chest. Revealing herself to him, giving herself totally to him. The thoughts running through her mind made her body yearn for action.

"Stephanie?" She heard sounds that seemed familiar to her. "Stephanie? Hello! Are you okay?" Caleb was calling her name. Damn, had she said or done anything that would let him know where her thoughts were? "Yes." "Are you okay? I have been calling your name for a few seconds now." "Yeah, I am fine. What did you need?" "Okay, you had me worried for a minute. Are you sure you are okay?" "Yeah, I am good. What's up?" "How do you feel about rowboats?" "I am good with them." "Great, would you like to go out on the water?" "That sounds like a plan." They walked over to the rowboat, got in, and Caleb rowed. In no time, they were far out in the water. Caleb put the ores in the boat and grabbed the backpack again. He pulled out a small tablecloth and placed it on the bottom of the rowboat. Had her attention now. She watched as he pulled out some wine glasses, cheese, prosciutto, paper plates, and wine. He rolled the prosciutto around the cheese and handed a piece to Stephanie. While she waited in amazement, he poured her a glass of Moscato. He prepared the same thing for himself. When he had all he needed, he raised his glass and said, "Beauty is in the beholder's eye, and I behold you. Here is to many more beautiful moments between us!" She smiled, leaned over, and gave him a kiss. They both took a sip of their wine, then ate their prosciutto and cheese. He had just introduced her to the romantic side of Caleb. He hoped to impress her so she would want to spend much more time with him. He knew he wanted to spend a lot more time with her. He had known it since he was first assigned to her case. Now he had the pleasure of being in her company, not for business, but on a personal level. That was what he had wanted since he first laid eyes on her. That was why he made sure he had twenty-four-hour surveillance on her. He had to make sure that nothing would happen to her. On his watch, nothing would ever get close enough to harm her!

She laid back, looked up at the sky, and just took it all in when she had finished eating. Caleb had really impressed her. She was more than grateful that he went through so much effort for her. Although her body wanted to thank him more pleasingly, her mind told her to thank him differently. "Caleb, thank you so much for this; I really appreciate it. This was much more than a simple walk!" "Stephanie, you are so welcome. I wanted you to really enjoy yourself." As she lay there looking up at the sky, he rowed the boat back to shore. The movement of the boat, coupled with the beautiful sky, made her feel like she was in heaven. She had experienced nothing like this before. None of her previous dates had ever been this thoughtful. He really outdid her expectations. And to think, she almost declined to go for a walk with him. She now knew that Caleb could be full of beautiful surprises. She let out a slight laugh. "What's so funny?" "A walk. Really? You are something else. I have to watch you, Mr. Caleb." "Ah, so you are interested?" "Yeah, I am damn sure interested!"

Chapter 50

A little after two in the morning, Cashmere walked through the door. Simeon had fallen asleep on the couch with his notepad on his chest. She smiled because he looked so comfortable lying there. Saw the pad lying on his chest and, for a quick second, thought about picking it up and reading it. Then she remembered how serious he had been earlier about his music. She decided to just leave it there and not make matters worse. She would already have to make up for not picking him up at the airport. Especially since it seemed as if he would not let it go.

She went to the bedroom, pulled back the sheets, then went into the bathroom to freshen up. After she was done, she returned to the living room and nudged him a little until he stirred. "Baby, come on, let's go to bed!" He took a minute to understand. Finally, she pulled him up, and he realized she was home. They went to the bedroom, he got under the covers, and he was snoring before she could get in the bed. She lay there and watched him for a few seconds, wishing he was still awake.

The morning sun shone through the bedroom window, catching Simeon's face. He stirred. When he awoke, he looked to her side and didn't see her. "Cashmere, where are you?" She came into the bedroom with a cup of coffee.

"I was wondering when you would wake up, sleepy head." "What time is it? How long did I sleep?" "It's almost 11:30am. I have lunch for us." "Lunch would be nice, but I must get ready. I am supposed to be in the studio in an hour." "The studio again? When are we going to spend time together, Simeon?" "You know I came to work on some of my music." "Studio time, is that all you came for?" "No, but I have to take care of business." She looked at him with much attitude. "You know what, Cashmere, don't get to tripping. We could have spent time together last night, but you rolled out with your girls." "Oh, so now it is my fault?" "It's not about whose fault it is. It's about we both have other obligations." "Whatever, Simeon. Go to the damn studio!" She walked out of the bedroom, slamming the door behind her. A few seconds later, he heard a lot of noise. Dishes are being thrown in the sink, and cabinets slamming. He figured lunch had been thrown away. Damn, why didn't he wait until after he had eaten to tell her? He jumped in the shower, put on his clothes, opened the door slowly, and walked out. She was in the living room, watching t. v., with an evil look on her face. "I'll be back later on, Cashmere." "Whatever," she said as he was walking out the door. She stared at the door, burning a hole in it with her eyes. She was on fire; her anger had reached an all-time high. It was probably best he left when he did. Had he stayed, he would have seen how foul she could be. She knew he wasn't ready to see that.

Hell, no one was ready for all that. Had to get herself together. Didn't want to still have all this anger when he returned. She did the one thing that always made her feel better. She went to Lil Ingrid's room, who was still fast asleep. All she had to do was just look at her, and things would instantly improve. Lil Ingrid brought a smile to her face. She could feel her anger subsiding within her.

She knew that Simeon was still trying to make her pay for not picking him up at the airport. What she didn't know was how long he would make her pay for it. The question was how long she would put up with it. Cashmere didn't do well with arguing unless she was the one doing the arguing. However, she didn't react to Simeon as she reacted to everyone else. He had a hold on her or something. He made her think about things differently. It's like he brought out a slightly better side of her or something. She wasn't sure if she was on board for all that, though. She enjoyed being the intimidating, mouthy, no-bullshit Cashmere. She had worked a long time to perfect her reputation. It wasn't the time for anybody to see her as weak or average. Simeon really didn't know her or how she could be. She hadn't unleashed her wrath on him because she didn't have a reason to. If he kept this foul act up for longer, he would definitely be privy to it.

Her plan was to wait for him to return and see how his mindset was. If he was over it and cool about things, she would make the night interesting for both of them. If he was still tripping, things would definitely heat up, not in a good way. Several hours sped by, and he hadn't made it back yet. He must have been swamped in the studio. Hopefully, he will finish the song tonight and won't have to return. She wanted him to herself before he had to go back to New York.

She had known Simeon for a few months, but their relationship hadn't progressed as she had hoped. It was partly due to him living in NYC and partly due to their not really pursuing one another the way she had hoped. When he was in New York, he hardly called her. Only when he was supposed to come to Virginia for studio time would she hear from him. At that moment, it clicked for her. Simeon wasn't really into her. He was using her for a place to stay while he was in town. She couldn't believe that she hadn't figured it all out before. Her mind had been so clouded with what she thought was going on between them that it had distorted her sense of reality. Simeon was playing a game with her! Damn, she felt so stupid for not seeing it sooner. He hadn't even tried to touch her the whole time he had been there. She figured that it was because he was mad; he wasn't interested in her like that anymore. Damn, what was she to do?

Should she let him back in the house and tell her how she felt? Should she leave him out there to figure things out for himself?

She had options, but which one was the right one to choose? One thing is for sure she had plenty of time to think about it. He probably wouldn't return until late tonight. Then, when he did, he would claim to be too damn tired and go to sleep. Just thinking about it made her blood boil. The more she thought about it, the madder she became. It was a good thing he wasn't with her right now. He would get a piece of her mind, that's for sure.

The evening eased into the night. So many hours had passed, and he still hadn't returned. Cashmere had fallen asleep on the couch, waiting for his return. She got up when she heard a knock on the front door. "Yes?" "Baby, open the door." "For what?" "What do you mean for what? So I can come in, that's why." "Simeon, there really isn't a need for you to come in here anymore." "What the hell are you talking about?" "I'm talking about the fact you really aren't into me. You only contact me when you need to come to town to work on your music." "Cashmere, you are tripping. Open the door, please." "I don't think so, Simeon. I think I have opened the door far too many times for you. It's time I stop doing that." "This is ridiculous. Can I at least get my stuff?"

"Yeah, you can get your stuff." "Open the damn door, so I can get it then." "There isn't a need for that?" "Why is that?" "Because Simeon, your shit is sitting on the back porch. Good night!" Just like that, she walked away from the door, turned off the living room light, and went to bed! She had just walked away from Simeon!

Chapter 51

"Babe, did you have a good time last night?" "Yes, I did, Rico. Thanks for making it a great night!" "No problem, I would do anything to see you smile." "You are so sweet. I wanted to talk to you about something, though. I am so sorry that our anniversary slipped my mind." "It's all good, baby. We spent it doing what we both love. As long as we were together, that's all that matters." "Are you sure? I would understand if you felt some kind of way about it." "I am sure. Besides, we have many more anniversaries to celebrate. Right?" There was a slight pause, then "Yes, we definitely have many more to celebrate."

Tammy just leaned in and gave Rico a kiss. He was good to her. She was lucky to have him. She had expected him to react differently about the whole anniversary thing. But, surprisingly, he was cool with it.

Rico felt some way about it, but he let it go. He realized that there would be many more anniversaries to celebrate with her. This one could slide this time. The next anniversary would definitely be one to celebrate, especially if things went as he hoped. He knew he had something special with her. She was someone he could grow with and would definitely complete him. Rico knew she was the one for him, and he was the one for her.

It was time to let her know just how much he wanted her. He checked the time on his phone and noted that he had about seven hours before he would put his plan in motion. Everything was set. All that was needed was to have her in place. But he still needed to complete that part.

"Babe, I will be back in a little while; I need to run errands." "Okay, Tammy, when do you think you will return?" "I shouldn't be too long. Maybe a couple of hours." "Okay, hurry back. Not sure how long I can withstand being without you." She smiled. "You can be so corny sometimes, Rico." "I know; that's why you love me, though." "I guess. Okay, I will see you later." She walked out the door. Now he had time to get her clothing together. He had purchased her dress, shoes, and accessories for the evening. Hopefully, she would find them as stunning as he did. When he saw them, he instantly realized that the outfit was meant for her.

His suit was on point too. He had picked out his tie and handkerchief to match her dress. Hell, even his cufflinks matched her dress. He needed to have everything in place in enough time she could get ready. They needed to be out the door by six forty-five at the latest.

Her keys twisted in the lock, and she was back. It was perfect timing too. It was time for him to get her a glass of Moscato. She walked into the kitchen looking wonderful. "This is for you, baby," he handed her the wineglass. "Thank you, baby." She walked away, heading to the living room. Damn, she looked good. She smelled good too. He wanted to take her right then and there. She didn't have a clue what the night would bring for her. He grabbed a glass of vodka and cranberry juice and headed into the living room with her. She had turned on the television for a bit of entertainment. He sat down beside her and touched her leg. She looked at him with a smile. He kissed her on her neck. Damn, she smelled wonderful. He couldn't help but want to kiss her more. He knew that if he went there with her, it might make it challenging to make their appointment on time. Besides, hopefully, there will be plenty of time for that tonight. Hopefully, there will be something to celebrate!

"Babe, I think I will take a shower. Did you want to take one after me?" She looked at him. "Baby, are you trying to tell me something? Do I need to take a shower now?" "Well, to be honest, I would like you to take one." She kept looking at him. "Well, if I need to take one, I will do just that." "Great, thank you, babe! Finish your wine, and I will be back soon." Rico went to the bathroom and jumped in the shower. He knew she was wondering what was going on.

She would know exactly what was going on soon. Rico was done showering; he wrapped the towel around him and went to the living room to get her. "Babe, I left the water running for you." "Okay, I will be in there in a minute." He went back to the bedroom, and she followed soon behind him. Kissing him on the cheek, she got in the shower. The whole time she wondered what he had planned. The one thing she knew about Rico was that when he did something, he went all out. So tonight had to be something special. Once he heard the shower door close, he pulled out her outfit for the evening, placing everything on the bed. He stood there, looking over everything to ensure he hadn't forgotten anything. She would be out soon, so he wanted to ensure everything was in place. The dress, the shoes, and the accessories were all displayed to her surprise. Then, he heard the water stop. She will be out soon.

A few minutes later, the bathroom door opened. She walked out, and her eyes went straight to the bed, then to him. "Babe, what is this? What is going on?" "Babe, please put this on. We have plans for tonight." She couldn't help but smile. He had made sure she had something spectacular to wear for whatever he had planned. She put on her clothes, and he pulled out his clothing and got dressed. By the time he was dressed, she was almost done. Once she was done, she looked at him, smiled, and adjusted his tie.

"You clean up nicely, Mr. Rico," "As do you, Ms. Tammy!" "So, what are we doing tonight?" "You will see. I hope that you will have a great time." "Would you like another glass of wine?" "If you're having something else, I will take one." "Sounds good." He went into the kitchen, glanced at the clock, poured two more drinks, then patted his suit pocket to ensure he had the ring. When he returned, she was sitting on the couch, looking even more stunning than he had imagined. Her beauty distracted him. He held the glass while he gazed at her. "Rico? Rico?" "Sorry, here you go, baby." She laughed and took the wine glass. He raised his glass to hers, "Here's to a great night with my baby! Cheers." "Cheers." Just as they were finishing up their drinks, the doorbell rang. When he opened the door, she heard, "Hello, your limo is here." He turned to Tammy, held out his hand, and said, "Shall we?" She took his hand and let him lead her to the limo. The chauffeur opened the door for them. She got in first. Rico walked around to the other side and got in. When he looked over at her, she said, "Rico, what are you up to?" "Nothing." "Yeah, okay. This doesn't seem like nothing." "Excuse me, driver, could we please have music? Something romantic, please." The driver turned on some slow romantic music, closed the partition, and pulled off. Tammy kissed Rico on the cheek.

"What was that for?" "It is for whatever you have planned for tonight. Thank you if I am too overwhelmed to do it later." All he could do was smile, for he knew exactly what she was in store for. Tammy looked out the tinted window to figure out where they were headed. That's when Rico noticed and pulled her close to him. Kissing her to try to take her mind off of trying to find out their destination. The driver made a left, a right, and two more lefts. Rico placed kisses all along her neck. She knew exactly what he was doing, but it felt far too good to her to try to stop him. Besides, she didn't want him to stop! He knew just the right places to kiss her. He knew exactly what he was doing to her. Then, just as she was getting into it, the limo stopped. "Oh baby, we're here," Tammy just looked at him. "You know that's not right!" The driver opened the passenger side, so Tammy could get out first. Rico slid across the seat after her.

There was a line out the door. People were waiting to get a table. Rico reached for her hand and guided her up to the door. "Right this way, sir, I believe your table is in order." They followed the doorman as he escorted them to the maitre d'. "Awe, right on time. Follow me!" The maitre d' lead them to a table in the back of the restaurant, right by the kitchen. "Please be seated! Your waiter will be right with you."

When the waiter arrived, he had a bottle of champagne and sat it on the table. After pouring their glasses, he said, "Enjoy your evening," then walked away. "Um, wasn't he supposed to take our order, baby?" "Yes, he was. I'm not sure what's going on here." "Good evening, welcome to Rains. I'll be taking care of you tonight," Stephanie said. "I thought you weren't working tonight," Rico said. "I wasn't, but I decided to come in and take care of some things. How is the champagne?" "It is delicious, thanks." Tammy looked at Stephanie with a curious look on her face. Stephanie smiled and asked, "May I take your order, or would you like a few more minutes?" "Tammy, would you mind if I ordered for us?" "Not at all, Rico. Go right ahead," "The lady will have the southwestern maple glazed salmon with pineapple salsa, asparagus, and cheesy risotto. I will have the grilled spice rubbed; tenderloin with chimichurri, garlic mashed potatoes, and roasted

Brussel sprouts, please." "Nicely done, Rico, Tammy said." "I will get that order in for you two." Stephanie refreshed their glasses with champagne before she left to place their order. "How could we get this table with all those people outside waiting to get in?" "Babe, you know Stephanie will take care of us. She wouldn't make us wait in that long line. That's your girl!" "I know. I feel bad, knowing that all those people were here before us."

"That's very nice of you, but please believe, if they could be in our shoes, they would be. Besides, we had reservations." "I guess you're right, Rico. They should be so lucky." "It's all about planning for what you want, baby! All about taking the necessary steps to accomplish what you desire." "You are so right. Most people don't plan like they should." A few minutes later, Stephanie returned with their dishes. She placed them in front of them. "Please enjoy. Let me know if I can get you anything else." "Thank you, Stephanie. It all looks so tasty," Tammy said. They toasted before they ate. "To a wonderful person I am very fortunate to be in love with!" Rico said with a huge smile. Tammy blushed and rubbed his hand.

By the time they had finished their dinner, Tammy was all smiles. "That meal was sheer perfection. You really did a great job picking dinner, babe!" "Thank you, babe, but that's not all. I did a great job at picking. Rico looked up towards the kitchen and nodded to the waiter.

A few seconds later, Stephanie returned with a plate with a round metal cover and placed it in the center of the table. She refreshed their champagne and picked up the other dishes. "Do you remember when I said it's all about taking the necessary steps to accomplish what you desire?"

"You said it a few minutes ago." "Well, babe, I ordered you a special dessert. I hope you like it!" Tammy looked at him. Rico placed his hand on the metal cover. When he lifted the metal cover, she saw a black box. Rico took her hand, "Tammy, you are the greatest person I have ever met. I desire you for the rest of my life! Will you marry me?" Rico opened the box and saw a breathtaking diamond before her. She paused for a few seconds, which seemed like an eternity to Rico. "Yes! Yes! Yes, I will marry you, Rico! Yes!!!!!"

Chapter 52

The following day Stephanie was awakened by a call from Caleb. "Good morning," she said in a groggy voice. "Good morning to you as well. I am sorry if I woke you up." "It's okay; I needed to get up anyway. What's going on?" "Well, I am in your neighborhood; I was wondering if you wanted to cook breakfast for us?" "Cook breakfast for us? Is that your way of inviting yourself over?" "Well, not really. Kind of, sort of. Okay, yes!" I'll tell you what, I had a rather late night last night. Why don't we meet for lunch in a few hours? I think I would prefer that." "I was trying to get a chance to see you in your pajamas." "Who says I wear pajamas? And if I did, what makes you so sure that I would let you see them?" "Well, I was hoping you would be nice since we had such a great time the other night." "Oh, I am very nice. I don't think we are at the stage where you see me in my pajamas.

You have to put in some more work to get there." "Stephanie, you drive a hard bargain. I'll play along, though. Lunch it is then." "Just to be fair, meet me at the restaurant at 12:30, and I will make you a great lunch." "Are you sure? I can take you out to lunch too." "Yeah, I'm sure. I have some work to do before the dinner service starts." "Oh, this is about work? I see." "It is about seeing you and getting my work done too. I have to keep grinding if I want this place to be the best restaurant in Richmond. I am sure you can understand that." "Yeah, I understand, but all work and no play make for a boring life." "True, but all play and no work makes for an unsuccessful life." "Okay, let's do lunch, but the next date, I get to have you all to myself. No work, no friends, Just you and me. Deal?" "Possibly! We'll have to see about that." "I guess that is better than a "No." "Last time I checked, it was."

"Okay, I will see you at Rains at 12:30 sharp." "Great, see you then." Stephanie hung up the phone and started laughing. She enjoyed playing hard to get with him. Knowing he wanted her, Stephanie also desired him. She just wasn't ready to give herself to him yet. So she was keeping him at bay for now. He could be very charming. He was definitely confident. Sometimes she thought his confidence was superb. Other times, she thought he was just being cocky. To her, there was a thin line between the two. Caleb didn't have a clue as to how she felt about his confidence slash cockiness. If things worked out between them, she would eventually tell him about it. If they didn't, then it wouldn't matter anyway.

She jumped in the shower, toweled herself dry, and then made some much-needed coffee. She needed that caffeine to jumpstart her day. It would indeed be a long one. After her lunch with Caleb, she needed to edit the daily special menu. She was also expecting a produce order that would be needed for tonight's dinner. The restaurant was doing great. Rains was filled to capacity almost every time it was opened. Business would be booming tonight. Stephanie had to hire more staff to accommodate all the guests who loved eating at her establishment. Her bar was always busy with people waiting for tables; there were always somewhat lengthy wait times. People just seemed to keep coming. The food was great, and the atmosphere was even more remarkable. It just so happened that tonight was a special night for a couple of her patrons. Her parents were celebrating their thirty-fifth wedding anniversary. Thirty-five years of loving one another. Her parent's relationship was anything but perfect. Lord knows that they have had their trials and tribulations. However, the one constant thing is the love they share. Nothing else seemed to even matter because their love would always be the glue that held their relationship together!

It was about 11:45. Caleb would be walking through those doors in forty-five minutes. She still needed to change the daily specials menu, and the produce shipment hadn't arrived yet. Decided to just start on the menu since only a couple of changes needed to be made. By the time Caleb walked through the door, she had just put the finishing touches on the menu. One of the waitresses brought him to the kitchen. He looked at her and gave her the biggest smile she had ever seen. "You're smiling like you haven't seen me in forever." "I'm smiling like it is so wonderful to see you again! I can't wait to try this delicious lunch you have prepared for us." "Is this visit about me or the food?" "Honestly, it is about both. Mainly about you, though, the food is an added bonus." "That is a good answer." "Yeah, I'm quick on my feet!" "That's good to know. I'll keep that in mind." "Here's something else you should keep in mind." He leaned in and gave her a little kiss on the lips. "What was that for?" "Something to keep on your mind until the next one!" "When will the next one be?" "We can work on it right now if you want?" "I want, but maybe we should wait until we are in a more private setting." "Just tell me when and where, and I am there." "We can talk about it over lunch." She placed two plates on the counter for them. He looked at the plate in front of him and said, "That looks amazing! I'm glad it's for me." "I'm glad you think it looks amazing. I hope it tastes as amazing as it looks." She reached down for his fork, scooped some food on it, and said, "Try this first." He opened his mouth, and she slid the fork in until he pulled the food off of it. She waited a few seconds to let him get the fullness of the flavor. He smiled and just looked at her. That's when she knew the flavors had kicked in, and he was enjoying them. "Stephanie, I don't know how you made this, but I definitely want some more," She took a forkful from her plate and let the flavors linger for a few seconds before she swallowed it. "You can have as much as you would like. There is plenty." "Good, 'cause sometimes I can have an insatiable appetite." "It's a good thing I own a restaurant then. There should be enough food in this place to satiate your appetite." Smiles emerged from both of them.

Stephanie cleared their plates and scraped the little bit left in the trash can; she went over to the sink and washed them, then dried them and set them in a pile with the others. Caleb watched her the whole time as if he couldn't take his eyes off her. She could be feisty sometimes, but he seemed to be drawn to that. She was anything but predictable. He never knew which way her comments would lend themselves. She could be sweet as sugar or explosive as a molotov cocktail. "What's on your mind, Caleb? Why are you so quiet?" "Just taking it all in." "Taking what all in?" "You! That's what. You are truly something else." "I hope you mean that as a compliment, Caleb." "It could never be anything else!"

"So, what about this next date," Caleb asked. "Well, what did you have in mind, Caleb? "I was thinking about this Saturday. There is a place that I really want you to see." "Where is this place? What is this place?" "I would rather not say. I want it to be a surprise!" "A surprise, huh? Those can go either way. They can be a good or a bad thing." "Well, let's hope for the former." "Yeah, let's hope for the former. What time Saturday?" "May I pick you up at noon?" "Sure, noon is fine." "This better be good, Caleb." "You sound as if you may have some doubts." She laughed, then said, "Just giving you a hard time!" "I see. It's all good, though. Okay, I have imposed on you long enough. I know you have work to do. May I call you later tonight?" "Thanks for having lunch with me. Yes, let's talk later on tonight. That would be really nice." Caleb got up, hugged Stephanie, and started to walk away. "Umm, Caleb " "Yes?" "What? No kiss before you leave?" "Oh, we can definitely do that." He walked back over to her, pulled her close, looked into her eyes, and kissed her soft sensuous lips.

Chapter 53

Maybe it was time for Stephanie to allow Caleb to be around more in her life. She was enjoying his company. His kisses weren't bad, either. After he left, she realized she was excited to see him. It disappointed her to see him go.

Cashmere had blocked Simeon's number; his calls were relentless over the past couple of weeks. She wasn't trying to talk to him. Didn't even want to hear his voice. She tried her best to put him out of her mind. Something inside of her made her think about him, though. She missed him more than she thought she would.

Tammy was still reeling over Rico's proposal. It truly surprised her. She couldn't take her eyes off of her breathtaking ring. Rico had really chosen a great ring to propose to her with. Next, she had to get together with her girls. They needed to see that he had put a ring on it. She grabbed her phone and sent a group text.

Tammy... Hey ladies, how is everyone doing?

Stephanie... Things are well; how are you?

Char... Been busy getting this fashion line out there. How are you?

Cashmere... Been okay. How about y'all?

Tammy... Doing great! We should all get together soon.

Char... I am free this Friday.

Cashmere... So am I.

Stephanie... I can do Friday too.

Tammy... Let's meet up at my place around 7. Is that good for everyone?

Cashmere... Sounds good; see you then.

Stephanie... Me too.

Char... Okay, I'll be there.

Char placed her phone down, only to hear it buzz again. This time it was her assistant, texting about a fabric issue. Apparently, there was a mixup in the fabric she ordered for her new design. If they couldn't get this fabric issue handled in time, it would set them back at least a week which wouldn't be the end of the world; it would make things a little stressful. Char just likes to make sure that everything runs smoothly. There was never a dull moment in the fashion world for her. Every accomplishment seems to always be a catastrophe waiting in the wings. Her phone buzzed again. It was her assistant again; she could correct the fabric mixup. Everything was back on track, crisis averted.

Friday crept up on everyone. It couldn't have come at a better time, either. The girls needed some girl time. No more work, no men, no family members, just the four of them and some great conversation.

The doorbell rang promptly at 7pm. Char, Cashmere, and Stephanie were all standing there when Tammy opened the front door. "Come on in, ladies!" Tammy hugged them one by one as they entered her home. Although they had just spent time together recently, they always seemed to act like they hadn't seen one another in years. Their bond was immeasurable. They followed Tammy to the kitchen, where Moscato was waiting for them.

Tammy had prepared light snacks of cheese, pepperoni, prosciutto, and crackers for them to munch on. Stephanie filled their glasses with wine. They all raised their glasses in the air, "To true friends now and forever!"

Char said. "I know that's right," Cashmere said. "Come, ladies, let's go into the living room. So, what's been going on since we last saw one another?" Tammy asked. "I'll start. Well, there has been a certain someone I have been spending time with. And let me tell you, I am enjoying his company!" Stephanie said with a massive smile on her face. "Do tell, don't leave out the juicy details. You know we want to know!" Cashmere said. Char and Tammy shook their heads in agreement. "Okay, well, we have gone out on a couple of dates, and they have been rather interesting. He is a cool guy and charming to boot." "Um, is that the juicy stuff? Because if it is, I'm still thirsty for more!" Cashmere said as she laughed a little. "Stop it, Cashmere. He is really a nice guy, and I like him. He makes me laugh and seems to crave spending time with me!"

"Speaking of spending time with someone or the lack thereof. Simeon and I are no more. Seemingly only wanted to talk when he was in town. And when he comes to town, all he wants to do is go to the studio to work on his music. Oh yeah, and crash at my place when he's done. I guess he found me to be a bed-and-breakfast of some sort. I had to let him know that he had to go." "What made you think he was using you?" Char asked. "Well, he would sleep until he had to get up to go to the studio. He would stay there all day and night and return well in the morning. He'd just get in the bed and go to sleep." "You mean you guys didn't even," Stephanie asked. "Well a couple of times, but that was when I was in New York. When he came here, all he had time for was the studio. Ladies, don't think I didn't try either. He wasn't interested anymore. So, he had to go! Let him find another woman to be his bed-and-breakfast 'cause this one isn't having it!" "Damn Cashmere, I am so sorry he didn't work out. He seemed like a nice guy too," Tammy said. "Well, I should have known; when I met him, it was about music. I should have realized that he was married to his music, and I wouldn't come first." "I guess it wasn't meant to be," Char stated. "It's all good. My focus should really be on Lil Ingrid, anyway. He is a distraction that kept me from giving her all my attention."

"Ladies, let me tell you the great news at From My Mother's Closet! We have just secured our first cover in a national magazine. From My Mother's Closet will take the world by storm. Next month my crew and I are flying to Milan to premiere our new line of handbags. Things have really been taking off for us! I am so glad that this clothing line is doing well. It has been a long road to get here. When I decided to retire from modeling, I wasn't sure if I could pull this off. So many nights, I wondered if I had made the right decision. The one thing I knew was that if I didn't give up and stayed the course, I could make it happen. It's like my mother always told me, "You can do anything you put your mind to!" She was definitely right about that; her words have always resonated with me. I would recall them at many points throughout my life. They fueled my desire and determination to be the best I could be!" "That is great, Char! We are thrilled for you," Cashmere said.

"Tammy, what's going on with you, girl? You have been mighty quiet over there," Stephanie said. "I've just been listening to everyone's stories. I have news, though. So, Rico and I went out the other night. He took me to this very nice restaurant. You may have heard of it. It is called 'Rains.' Stephanie smiled! We had a delicious dish our very own sister, Ms. Stephanie, prepared! The best champagne in the house! I tell you, the night was surely the best we had ever encountered together. Rico was just amazing! And then, it happened. They placed this small plate covered with a metal bowl on the table. I wasn't sure what it was. He said something about a special dessert.

Rico looked at me, reached over, and lifted the metal bowl off the plate. Underneath the napkin was a black box! He opened the box, and I saw the most exquisite diamond ring ever. He asked me to marry him right there at Rains!" "And you said," Stephanie asked. "You know exactly what I said! I said, 'Yes, Yes, Yes!'" Tammy pulled out the stunning diamond to show her girls! "That is amazing, our girl is getting married! I guess I'll be a bridesmaid," Char said. "Bridesmaid, hell, I will be the maid of honor," Cashmere blurted out. "I tell you what, It is fantastic to know that we are all doing well and still close after all these years, Stephanie said." "Ladies, you know nothing can break this bond of sisterhood," Char said with a huge smile.

Just then, Cashmere's phone rang. "Hold on, I have to take this." She stepped outside, "Hello," "Cashmere, Uncle Herbert here. When you get a chance, can you come to the store? I've reviewed the financials and noticed discrepancies I think we need to discuss!" Cashmere paused for a second as she tried to swallow the lump in her throat. "Cashmere, are you there?" "Yes, Uncle Herbert, I am here. Sure I will be there tomorrow. We can review the books together then!" "Come first thing in the morning, okay?" "Yes, first thing in the morning!" Cashmere hung up the phone. "Is everything okay," Tammy asked.

"Yeah, yeah! Everything is fine. I need to meet with Uncle Herbert tomorrow, that's all!" "Are you sure?" "Could you please pour me another glass of Moscato? I will be there in a few minutes." "Sure." Tammy walked back in, leaving Cashmere on the patio. Cashmere just hung her head in shame, for she knew precisely what Uncle Herbert would say to her tomorrow! Damn!

Until Next Time

Other Books by William Dance

Words From Me to You! (Poetry)

The Adventures of Boris and Friends
(Children's Book)

The Bonds of Sisterhood (Novel)

Coming Soon

FIXER

FIXER

Chapter 1

The alarm clock went off at 6:45 am. Crush rolled over and hit the snooze button. He knew he needed to get up, but 6:45 had come just too damn early. The alarm clock went off again at 6:50. Crush got up, brushed his teeth, showered, and put on his suit. Grabbed a boiled egg, a piece of toast, some orange juice, and his keys. Out the door he went, on his way to work. Today will be a busy day for him. He had several appointments he needed to attend. Crush pulled up to his first appointment of the day. His appointment was on time, 7:30am; the account exited the house and headed to his car. Pulled out of his driveway and went to the right. Crush followed him, turning up his music as he approached the light. Crush rolled down the window, and his appointment looked over at him. That was it bang bang went the 9mm. Two to the dome, his appointment fell over, and Crush pulled off. He drove to his favorite coffee shop and got his usual paper and coffee. He sat at a table, pulled out his phone, and pressed "Solo." The phone rang. "Solomon here; what's up, Crush?" "Met with my first appointment. Everything is taken care of." "Great!" Crush hung up the phone and read his paper. "Good morning." Crush looked up, wondering if someone was talking to him. "Hi! Over here." He looked over and saw a beautiful woman looking at him. "Good morning to you as well. How are you this morning?" "I am fine, thank you. How are you?" Crush got up and walked over to her table. "My name is Khiry, and you are?" "Hello Khiry, my name is Aja." "It is very nice to meet you, Aja. Might I add, Aja is a beautiful name. It seems to fit you." "Thank you, Khiry. You're not too bad yourself." "Thank you. I try to keep myself together." "It's working for you. Please join me if you would like." "Thank you, let me get my things, and I will be right back." Khiry walked over to his table to get his things. He returned to her table, sat down, and talked to Aja. Aja was exquisite. Short hair, light brown eyes, and sporting a curvaceous body on her chocolate-coated frame, just like he liked them. Khiry was much to her liking too. Hair twisted into strands, darkly coated like sweet dark chocolate. Sporting an athletic build. She could tell he took great care of his body. She couldn't help but smile at him. He returned the smile. She noticed his pearly whites, which was always a positive for her. She couldn't stand a man that didn't take care of his teeth. "I'm sorry, I have to cut this short. I have got to get to work." Aja said with a smile. "May I see your phone?" Khiry asked. "My phone? Why is that?" "I want to program my number in your phone, so you would have it if you wanted to see me again." "Very nice, but you come in every morning and get a paper and coffee," Aja said. "Oh, I have a stalker." "Not a stalker, maybe an admirer from afar. We'll continue this tomorrow." Aja said. With that, she got up and walked away. She could feel him looking at her. The truth is she welcomed his gaze. She threw a little something extra on her walk to give him something to remember. Khiry watched her until he couldn't see her anymore. She had his attention!

When Mr. Solomon got to the office, he had enough time to eat breakfast and turn on his computer before his first appointment. "Mr. Solomon, Andreas Johnson is here to see you." Kathy, his assistant, said. "Okay, Kathy, please take him to meeting room 'A.' I will be there in a few minutes." "Yes, sir, Mr. Solomon. Anything else, sir?" "Yes, please ensure refreshments are in the meeting room." "Yes, Mr. Solomon." Kathy led Mr. Johnson to the meeting room. "Please have a seat; Mr. Solomon will be with you shortly. I will bring refreshments for you to enjoy. Please don't hesitate to have something." "Thank you so much. I really appreciate it." Mr. Johnson said. "No problem, it's what we do here." With that, Kathy exited the meeting room to grab the refreshments that Mr. Solomon had requested. Mr. Solomon entered the meeting room and extended his hand. "Good morning! Mr. Johnson, I presume." "Yes, very nice to meet you, Mr. Solomon." "Likewise, Mr. Johnson." Kathy came in with refreshments. She placed coffee and bagels on the table between them. "Thank you, Kathy." Mr. Solomon said. She exited the meeting room, and Mr. Solomon spoke. "So, Mr. Johnson, how may I help you today?" "Well, Mr. Solomon. I was referred to you by one of my close friends. He said you helped him with a little problem he had." "Yes, I am in the business of solving problems. Please go on." "Well, I am having a little issue with my neighbor. He likes to frequent my home when I am not there." "Go on." "When my wife is alone, if you catch my drift." "Okay, so your wife is sleeping with your neighbor. How can I help you?" "Well, I would like for him to get the message." "What type of message do you want him to get?" "Put it like this I want him to be no more!" "Oh, I see. Well, something like that could be expensive. Are you financially prepared for such an investment?" Mr. Johnson opened his briefcase full of stacks of hundreds. "I would say money is not an issue Mr. Solomon." "That looks like a nice retainer. I would need pictures, addresses, and time frames." "I can get you all of that. Should I send them to your office?" "Oh no, sir. Please send nothing. We don't need a paper trail. You can drop it off, or we can meet. Let me know when you have everything, and we will go from there." Mr. Johnson closed his briefcase and got up to leave. "Mr. Johnson, you can leave half the money now, and I will collect the rest after the job is done." "Are you sure? This is one million dollars." "Yeah, I am sure. I will have Kathy take care of the retainer for you. Once you get me the information, I will let you know when everything will go down." "Great, I will have all that for you within the next week." "Sounds good, Mr. Johnson. We will talk to you soon. Enjoy the rest of your day." Mr. Johnson exited the meeting room. "Have a great day, Mr. Johnson, Kathy said." "Thank you, you too, Kathy." Mr. Solomon poured coffee and awaited his next appointment. "Kathy, could you please come in here for a moment?" Kathy entered the meeting room. "Yes, Mr. Solomon." "Kathy, could you please take care of this retainer for me? What time is my next appointment?" "Mr. Solomon, your next appointment is in twenty minutes." "Great, thanks. I will be in my office until then." They both headed away from the meeting room. Mr. Solomon was walking behind Kathy. "Kathy, you look very nice today." Kathy stopped, turned to face him, and said, "Thank you, Mr. Solomon, so do you." Mr. Solomon smiled at Kathy and walked on to his office. Kathy smiled as she watched him head to his office. She went to her desk and took care of the retainer as Mr. Solomon had asked her to do. "Kathy, please do me a favor and research, Mr. Johnson. Let me know what you find out about him." "Most definitely, sir. Mr. Domingo has just arrived, sir." "Thank you, please see him in meeting room A. I will be there soon." Mr. Solomon finished up the paperwork he was working on before going to the meeting. Mr. Domingo ate a bagel and drank coffee when he got to the meeting room. "Good morning Mr. Domingo; I hope you are doing well this morning." "I will do well if you give me some great news." Mr. Solomon grabbed a bagel and slid a folder over to Mr. Domingo. "Look at those." Mr. Domingo opened the folder and saw a man draped over a steering wheel at a stoplight. Mr. Domingo let a slight smile appear. "I take it you are pleased." Mr. Solomon said. "Yes, I am more than pleased. I am relieved. I feel like I have lifted a burden off my shoulders. This slime ball made my life miserable for over a year. I was at the end of my rope before I heard about you. He was blackmailing me and threatening to tell my wife of my infidelities. I couldn't lose my wife because of my stupidity." "Well, you don't have to worry about him anymore. He won't be bothering you again. Your secrets are your own again. Now, there's just the matter of settling your debt." "Of course, five hundred thousand, correct?" "Yes, that's correct. Five hundred thousand is due today." "Unfortunately, I don't have all five hundred thousand. I only have four hundred thousand." "No problem, Mr. Domingo. We will have Kathy set you up on a six-month payment plan. We totally understand how things can come up. We ask that you pay the debt off by the end of the sixth month. If not, then we will have to schedule another meeting. Understand!" "Yes, I understand, Mr. Solomon. I will pay it off ASAP." "Great, then we are on the same page." Mr. Domingo handed Mr. Solomon the briefcase with four hundred thousand dollars in it. Mr. Solomon opened the briefcase to inspect that the money was there. "Looks in line. Thanks again, Mr. Domingo. We will be in touch." Mr. Solomon grabbed the briefcase, left the meeting room, and handed the briefcase to Kathy. "Mr. Domingo will need to be on a sixth month's payment plan. Please advise him that he must have it paid by the last day of the payment plan, with no exceptions. If it is not paid by then, schedule an appointment with Crush for the next day." "Got it, Mr. Solomon. I will take care of everything." "I know you will, Kathy. That's why you're my right hand!" He smiled at Kathy and returned to the meeting room to finish with Mr. Domingo. "Mr. Domingo, everything is set. Please see Kathy on your way out for your payment plan. If you have any other issues or concerns, please contact us. We are always here for you and anyone you may know that would benefit from our services." He shook Mr. Domingo's hand and exited the meeting room. Mr. Domingo went to see Kathy for his payment plan. She gave him the instructions he needed to follow. He thanked her and agreed to everything she had stated. Mr. Domingo turned and left the office. It relieved him that his issue was taken care of, but now he had another issue. He had six months to come up with the rest of the money. He had already spent his life savings to pay Mr. Solomon for his services. Kathy was clear in her instructions, which let him know that he had better make good on his debt or he would have bigger problems.

Crush paid his bill and got in his car to meet his next appointment. He pulled up on time to see his appointment at the massage parlor. His weekly ritual. It's where he would enjoy his happy endings. Unfortunately, the end would be anything but happy today. The appointment was in his usual room, awaiting his regular masseuse. Crush opened the door; the appointment was lying face down on the table. "I have needed this all week, baby. Come on in here and do me!" "Be careful what you ask for!" Crush said. The appointment looked up to see the silencer of the 9mm pointed between his eyes. Bang, bang, went the gun. The appointment's head fell back to the table. The appointment just had an unhappy ending. Crush exited just as quickly as he had entered the parlor. He was back in the car rolling when his phone rang.

"Hello." Crush answered. "Crush, it's Kathy." "Hey Kathy, how are you?" "I am well, thanks. Just checking in to see how things are going?" "Things are going as scheduled. I met with my second appointment. Everything went as planned." "Great Crush. Mr. Solomon will be so pleased. Don't forget to come by at 2:00pm. Today, we are having cake and ice cream for Mr. Solomon's birthday." "Oh, that's right. I will be there. Thanks for the reminder." "You're welcome, Crush. See you then." "See you soon, Kathy."

Stay Tuned!!!!!